SHOWDOWN AT TRINIDAD

The big man knew that with no one left who could connect him with the train robbery, he was almost clear. No one, that is, except Frank Angel, special investigator for the US Justice Department. And Hainin realised that there was no stopping the lawman's pursuit. He might get away clear with the money, but Angel would never quit looking for him . . . never forget. It was a pity. But if Hainin was to ever know peace, Angel had to die!

Books by Daniel Rockfern
in the Linford Western Library:

BAD DAY AT AGUA CALIENTE

DANIEL ROCKFERN

SHOWDOWN AT TRINIDAD

Complete and Unabridged

LINFORD
Leicester

First published in Great Britain in 2007 by
Robert Hale Limited
London

First Linford Edition
published 2008
by arrangement with
Robert Hale Limited
London

British Library CIP Data

Rockfern, Daniel
   Showdown at Trinidad.—Large print ed.—
Linford western library
1. Western stories
2. Large type books
I. Title
823.9′2 [F]

ISBN 978–1–84782–243–7

Published by
F. A. Thorpe (Publishing)
Anstey, Leicestershire

Set by Words & Graphics Ltd.
Anstey, Leicestershire
Printed and bound in Great Britain by
T. J. International Ltd., Padstow, Cornwall

For pore ol' Angus

1

The train was carrying $250,000, and the three raiders got away with every cent of it.

Not that it was difficult.

She was a big old hayburner, belching a cloud of smoke that rose ten feet above the fluted stack and spitting sparks that smoldered in the thin grass alongside the tracks. You could hear her coming for ten miles or more in the slowly rising foothills to the south of Tularosa, her plume of smoke rolling back behind her like a billowing banner and wisping off to the west, where the long, yellow-white streak of the White Sands lay like strange water in the shadows of the San Andres Mountains.

The engineer braced his feet firmly on the cleated iron floor of the cab and leaned out on the right to see the long curve ahead that eased away from the black, basalt jumble of the *malpaís* toward Carrizozo, which was still hidden in the folding foothills of the Jicarillas ahead. The rushing wind cooled his skin heated dry by the blast furnace warmth of the open boiler, into which his stoker moved cord after cord of bundled wood, his black skin oiled with sweat, his muscles moving smoothly with the rhythm of his paced movement. Then the engineer ducked back in, cursing the stoker for not keeping the pressure — which had dropped infinitesimally on the huge clock dial in front of the engineer's face — up to its required level. The stoker took absolutely no notice at all of the steady stream of curses that the engineer was raining upon his unheeding head. His job was to put the wood in the boiler, and he was puttin' the wood in the boiler, and all the cussin' and yellin' in the world wasn't goin' to get the wood into the boiler no faster. Anyways, the engineer was like all the Southern Pacific's engineers, they cursed if the pressure was up, and they cursed if the pressure was down; and if it wasn't up and it wasn't down — why, they cursed just as loudly about that. A man might as well shake his fist at the rain, and Moses Glorification Washington wasn't fool enough to do that. So he kept up his steady rhythm, swinging the wood forward from the tender and onto the footplate, where it would dry out quickly before the open furnace, then sweeping it into the roaring hole with the long-handled shovel.

It was a short train, a special, just the loco, tender, and a caboose, with the two Pinkerton men guarding their not particularly special cargo. Not very special because, although the flimsy slatted box on the floor in the corner of the caboose contained a quarter of a million dollars, it didn't somehow seem like real money. It wasn't gold nor even silver bullion — not even fresh-minted greenbacks smelling of printing ink and secret desires. It was ruined money, tattered money, greasy, dirty, torn money on its way to the main branch of the First National Bank in Santa Fe to be burned. Standard procedure, although naturally enough, the banks didn't make a public relations exercise out of it. But federal greenbacks just couldn't take for very long the kind of treatment they got west of the Mississippi; They got creased, folded, wadded, and scrawled on — the result of being kept in the toes of boots rarely taken off and in belts frequently soaked with muddy river water. They got sewn into long johns which could probably have stood by their owners' beds unaided, and stuffed into sweatbands of Stetsons worn by men who spent most of their waking hours under a sun which could fry eggs on a flat stone. So every six months or so the government told the banks to call in old currency and replace it over the counter with new currency. The beaten, tired, limp, worn-out paper was then shipped to a specified head bank and destroyed under supervision.

In between, it was treated like trash, roughly bundled and packed into wooden crates such as chickens are often shipped in. It was guarded, if that was the right word, by some deputy marshal who fancied a train ride or, as in the case of this shipment, by two Pinkerton detectives returning east who didn't mind picking up an extra job and playing some penny-ante poker en route The slatted box they were guarding was, to them, worthless paper and would have still been so even if they had known that the banks had no record of even one serial number from any of the bundled notes nor any tally of where any of the bills had originated. They were just bundles of paper.

At least, they were until the raiders hit the train.

They took her in a gully just south of Carrizozo, using the time-honored technique invented by the Reno brothers and perfected by the James boys. A section of rail was unbolted, a lariat was looped under it, and the rail was yanked off the right-of-way — preferably, as in this case, just around a curve that would hide the damage until the engineer had only about three minutes to see the gap and slam on every ounce of brake he had.

And it worked like a charm.

The big old locomotive came bundling down the track, snorting like a fussy old buffalo during the mating season, and as the curve straightened, the engineer saw the missing rail and grabbed the huge brake lever, hauling it down with all his strength, hanging on to it and shouting curses at his Negro helper.

By the time Moses Glorification Washington knew what was wrong, the engineer, whose name was Pat Seele and who had been working for the Southern Pacific since he was twenty-four years old, had brought the train to a shuddering, screeching, panting halt, the drive wheels red-hot from the friction of the rails that had sent great showers of sparks leaping from under the locomotive. The wide cowcatcher was not more than ten feet from the place where the rail ran out, and Pat was halfway down the metal steps, cursing whatever blasted stupidity it was that had brought about this near-disaster when — as if from nowhere — a masked man came around the front of the train and stuck a Starr & Adams .38 under Pat's nose, his demeanor indicating that this was a bad day for heroics. Pat Seele took one squinting look at the pistol and then one at the cold eyes of the man holding it, and his hands went up as if someone had pulled strings attached to them.

'Who dat?' Moses shouted, coming to the side of the cab. 'Who dat down dere?'

'Shut your face and keep it shut!' snapped the man with the gun.

Moses nodded rapidly three times and backed up to let Seele climb into the cab. His eyes were wide, and his mouth hung open, but he made no overt move. The man with the Starr &

Adams smiled beneath the neckerchief covering his sallow face.

Almost before the train had come to a stop, two men had swung aboard the platform at the rear of the caboose, bursting open the door simply by kicking it hard. Since it had not been locked, the door smashed back lopsided on its hinges, and the two Pinkerton detectives, sprawled on the floor in the wreckage of their makeshift poker table by the sudden jerking halt of the train, looked up into the threatening muzzles of two short-barreled Colt revolvers, realized that their own coats — and pistols — were hanging on a hook behind the ruined door, and raised their hands as meekly as had the engineer.

'Up, up, up,' snapped the bigger of the two intruders. He was dressed in ordinary work clothes, blue denim pants, and woolen shirt. His hat was well pulled down to conceal his hair, and a bandanna across his face concealed everything else. The second man hustled the two Pinkertons to their feet and pushed them away, nearer to the big man, as he bent down to examine the slatted crate with the money in it.

'It's here,' he said, his voice muffled by the bandanna like that of his partner.

'Good,' nodded the first raider, and very quickly, quite ruthlessly, he knocked down the nearest of the two Pinkerton men with a vicious blow on the head from the barrel of his revolver. The second detective shrank back instinctively, making it that much easier for the second raider to drop him in precisely the same manner.

'Can you lift it?' the bigger man asked.

The other tested the weight of the crate, then swung it up. 'Just about,' he answered.

'Let me, then,' the first man said. 'Get down outside.'

As his partner swung down to the ground, he thrust his Colt into its holster and took hold of the crate with both hands. Muscles coiled visibly beneath the cheap work shirt, and he swung the heavy box easily around, walking through the broken door with it to the platform outside.

'Ready?'

'Ready.'

The man on the ground took the weight, and the other swung down beside him. He lifted the crate as the other man ran swiftly to the brush bordering the track and came back leading a pack mule. They lashed the crate very efficiently, very fast, onto the crosstrees on the animal's back, and then the shorter one gave a sharp, fluted whistle.

The man in the driving cab heard the whistle and gestured with the gun. Pat Seele and his stoker got warily down from the cab, their eyes on the gun, fear showing.

√ 'It's all right,' the man said. They could see him grinning beneath the mask. 'I ain't gonna shoot you.'

'Yessir,' Pat Seele said. 'Thank you.'

'Me an' my buddies are heading west,' the man said meaningfully. 'Understand?'

'Yessir,' Seele said again.

'Be sure you do,' the man said and spun on his heel, running to where the other two were already mounted on good-looking horses. He vaulted into the saddle of his horse already on the run, and the three of them turned across the tracks behind the train and moved off without haste toward the *malpaís*, which lay like a cicatrix on the earth perhaps four miles away. In fifteen minutes they were out of sight; Pat Seele didn't move until then.

'All right, boyo,' he said to Moses. 'Let's see what we can do for those Pinkerton fellers. Then we'll go find help.'

'Yassuh,' Moses said. 'Which way we go, find help?'

'Which way them bad men go, Moses?'

Moses looked at the sun for a moment and then counted on his

11

fingers. 'They went west, boss,' he responded.

'Which way you reckon we ought to go, then?'

Moses' smile was big and broad and warm and beautiful. 'East, maybe?'

'You bet your black ass!' answered Pat Seele.

2

The Department of Justice occupied a big old building on Pennsylvania Avenue at the corner of Tenth Street in Washington, D.C. It was far too small for the department's needs — something like a hundred and fifty people worked on the four floors it was allocated, although the use of the basement as an armory and facilities shared with the army's gymnasium helped a little. The attorney general, the man whose responsibility was the management of all aspects of the enforcement of law and order in the United States, had an office on the first floor, looking out over the bustling traffic on the wide avenue below. It was a spacious, high-ceilinged room with an anteroom outside for the attorney general's personal, private secretary, Miss Rowe, a honey blonde girl who only a few minutes before had shown Angus Wells, the chief investigator for the department, into the attorney general's office.

Wells now sat in the deep leather armchair opposite his chief, examining the room which was so much a reflection of the man and yet not really seeing it at all. It was as if he knew everything in it, as though each item were his own property and not that of the older man behind the desk. The shelves full of books, stacked every which way but tidy — upright and flat, spine out or face forward, books on law, criminology, on psychology, natural history, sociology, criminal jurisprudence, foreign law, land law, international law, all of them showing the wear of frequent use and the inability of their owner to treat them as anything but what they were: tools with which he did his work. The huge desk dominated the right-hand corner of the room, and two leather armchairs — one of which Wells occupied — were placed before it. The only other furniture was a heavy oak cupboard and an old-fashioned iron safe with a decorative brass scroll on the door. On the wall behind the desk and between the two floor-to-ceiling windows which looked out on the avenue was the circular seal of the department and the American flag.

'Angus,' the attorney general said, 'I don't know how I'm ever going to get started saying what I have to say.'

'Let me say it for you, then,' Wells said, his voice harsh. 'You want me to retire from active duty.'

He was a big man, Angus Wells, wide across the shoulders, athletically built. His face was tanned and healthy from outdoor living, and his blue eyes were as bright and inquisitive as a boy's. But when he stood, he no longer stood straight and tall. When he moved, he no longer moved with the cat-like speed and certainty that he once had. His once dark blond hair was now almost white, and his mustache, speckled with salt and pepper, made him look much older than the forty-eight years that were recorded in the manilla personal dossier that now lay on the attorney general's desk.

'Well, Angus . . . ' The attorney general spread his hands, seeking a way to say the right thing to this man, whom he liked so much and whose pride he could find no way to avoid hurting.

'Say it,' Wells said flatly. 'I'm not some sniveling kid!'

'All right, Angus,' the man behind the desk said. 'I had to look at your medical report. Standard procedure, you know that.'

'I know it,' was the unhelpful reply.

'Every six months,' the attorney general went on. 'It's not my rule.'

'I know that, too.'

'I was rough on you as it was, sending you down into New Mexico again so soon after the Cravetts business,' the attorney general said. 'But the medicos told me you'd made

16

such a great comeback, I let it go. You did a little pushing yourself, as I recall.' He tried to make it lighter, tried for a smile. Wells wasn't having any of that.

'Now this,' the AG said, tapping the folder in front of him. 'They couldn't take out the bullet you took in the back. It's lodged near your spine, and if you continue to engage in — oh, hell!' he ended, hopelessly, tossing the folder aside. 'Angus, they won't be responsible for what happens if you go on active service again. So there's nothing I can . . . I have to ask you to step down as chief investigator. Take yourself off the active roster.'

'Got any ideas what I can do?' Wells asked. 'Sell matches on street corners, maybe? Buy a wheelchair and get some pretty nurse to push me around?'

'Come on, man, you're being childish,' snapped the attorney general. 'You know damned well we need you in the department. You'll just have to take a desk job, that's all there is to it.'

'I don't want a desk job,' Angus Wells said.

'You don't have any choice, Angus.'

'Wrong. Sir.'

The attorney general looked up, a frown knitting his brows. He had hired Angus Wells himself, watched the man as he had proved his worth time and time again, meriting every commendation, every promotion, to his present rank as chief investigator. He had until now looked upon Angus Wells as a friend and confidant as well as an employee, and he hesitated to ask the next question because he knew and feared and did not wish to hear the answer. He asked anyway. 'Tell me why I'm wrong.'

'I can retire,' Angus Wells said.

'Yes,' nodded the attorney general, sighing. 'I have no way to stop you doing that. But I wish you would reconsider. I need you, Angus. I need your expertise — this blasted robbery in New Mexico, a quarter of a million dollars stolen! I . . . I ask you, as an old friend, as a personal favor to me — stay on.'

Wells let a chill smile touch his lips, and the attorney general was shocked to see contempt and dislike written plainly in the younger man's face. 'Let me ask you, as an old friend, as a personal favor,' Wells said, 'to keep me on active duty while I look into the New Mexico thing.'

The attorney general smacked a hand flat on the desk and got up from his chair, striding angrily across to the windows overlooking Pennsylvania Avenue, glaring down at the pedestrians and carriages without really seeing any of them. 'You know I can't, Angus,' he said.

'And you know I can't, either, Charles,' Wells replied softly, and for the first time his voice was touched with regret.

The attorney general nodded, sucked in his breath, and let it out as a long sigh. 'I suppose not,' he said. 'I suppose not.' He sat down, his shoulders slumping wearily. Absently he reached for the cigar-box to his right, taking one of the long black cigars and lighting it with a wooden match. His head wreathed in smoke, eyes crinkled to avoid flinching, he leaned back in the chair. 'When will you go?'

'Statutory four weeks,' Wells said. 'I suppose.'

'You'll not help with this New Mexico thing?'

'If I can,' Wells answered. 'But — '

'I know, I know,' the attorney general said, holding up a hand to forestall being told yet again. He didn't want to start thinking yet about how he was going to replace Angus Well's experience, wisdom, knowledge, and plain guts. He didn't want to start thinking, either, about what was wrong with a set of rules that declared a man a cripple and therefore unemployable in certain jobs when he had been crippled carrying out those jobs. He didn't want to give too much thought to how deep Angus Well's bitterness might go and whether — damn all political life! — his going meant the loss of another good friend.

'Could we at least talk about it?' he asked humbly.

'Sure,' Wells said. He didn't sound the least bit interested.

3

Morty Leaven had been with the Pinkerton Detective Agency for almost ten years, and he resented having been taken like an amateur. His partner, Ned Ruzzin, didn't feel any differently, and being a more vindictive man than his partner, was looking forward to laying hands on the cat who had laid the six-gun barrel alongside his skull, which was still throbbing as if someone were boiling water inside it.

Ruzzin was a big man, a burly man, well over six feet tall, with shoulders like oak beams and hands like hams. Leaven was shorter, squatter, older, smarter. Together, they were a pretty good team, highly thought of at the regional office in Denver.

After Moses Glorification Washington and Pat Seele had revived them by bathing their heads with tepid water from the engine, the two men held a council of war, which the engineer and his stoker had watched with wide eyes and puzzled expressions. They could not understand why Leaven and his partner clambered up on top of the caboose, looking from beneath eye-shading hands at the empty vastness around them. Leaven and Ruzzin didn't explain at first, either. They made their decisions, came to their conclusions, and discussed what they figured to do about both before they so much as even looked at the engineer and his helper.

Morty Leaven looked out across the lava beds with pursed lips, his eyes narrowed, thoughts busy. He knew this wild land, knew the bleak San Andres Mountains — and what lay beyond them.

'It doesn't figure,' he said to Ruzzin. 'Why would they head west? There's nothing out there for two hundred miles — and every mile of it Chiricahua country.'

Ruzzin nodded. Beyond the *malpaś*,

the lava beds, lay the empty San Andres Mountains and beyond them, the Jomada del Muerto, the wicked, bleached, lifeless area that the conquistadores had called the Death March. Arid, supporting no life, providing no water, containing no habitation, the Jomada was a place to be avoided like the plague.

'South'd be just as bad,' he put in, and Leaven nodded.

'White Sands down there,' he muttered, referring to the forty-mile-long stretch of dazzling white powdered gypsum and sand, where a horse would founder in drifts of shifting sand that blew like snow, scouring the skin off a man in a couple of hours if the wind came up and caught him out in the open. Sure, they could skirt the White Sands, climb the San Agustin, and drop down into Las Cruces, and then the Mexican border. But what for? Nobody knew who they were. The money they had stolen was untraceable. The way they had pulled the job meant that they knew both of those things. So they would not be trying to jump the border, and there was no reason for them to make a man-killing run across some of the most hostile country in the Southwest.

'Well over hundred and fifty miles to Santa Fe,' Ruzzin commented.

'And nothing to spend your money on when you get there,' Leaven replied.

He knew Santa Fe. That was the place the natives called the Americans *burros* — donkeys — and there wasn't a girl over ten that didn't have some kind of pox. The streets were nothing more than muddy alleys littered with the droppings of goats and chickens, and the only drink a man could buy was tequila. And between this point and Santa Fe — nothing. Literally, nothing. Oh, you could say there were a few villages, if you wanted to count huddled *jacales* like Belen as a village. You could say there were a few saloons, if you wanted to count the kind of deadfalls you'd find in Socorro. But that was all;

25

everything else was empty, rolling land, climbing mesas, falling canyons, dried-out runoffs, and bunch-grass that would just barely support the herds of goats the Mexicans kept on it.

Leaven pursed his lips again. These are smart boys, he told himself. They knew enough to pick a train carrying untraceable money — which might mean inside information. They knew enough not to talk any more than they had to. They knew enough to lay a false trail. Maybe they'd know enough to realize that any Pink worth his pay would expect them to do that and plump for the most likely route — which was north, ever north, keeping Gallinas Peak on your right, north past El Cuervo and Lamy, then up into Santa Fe. You could pick up Atchison Topeka & Santa Fe, you could hitch up with a wagon train returning empty across the Raton, you could head west to Arizona, north to Utah or Colorado, east into Texas, all comfortable distances from the territorial capital. Yes,

Santa Fe was the obvious place for them to go, and they were smart enough to know that he'd know that.

'I'm betting they headed east,' he said.

'I don't — ' Ruzzin began.

'Oh, they'll swing north for Santa Fe, all right,' Leaven said. 'But they won't go the way we expect. I'm goin' to put my money on them taking a run up into the Mescalero Reservation, across Lincoln County to the Pecos, follow the Pecos all the way on up to Glorieta if they like. It's easy country once you get across the mountains.'

'You could be right,' Ruzzin admitted. 'You could be awful wrong, too.'

'Hell, we just lost a quarter of a million dollars, Ned!' Leaven said. 'We sure as hell can't be any wronger than that!'

Ruzzin nodded ruefully.

'OK, Morty,' he said. 'Play her as she lays.'

'We'll head down track,' Leaven said. 'See if we can pick up some horses at

Oscuro. Then head up into the mountains. Hey, you, engineer!'

Pat Seele came over, and Morty Leaven told him about the conclusions he and his partner had reached and what they were going to do.

'It's about ten miles, give or take, down to Oscuro,' Leaven said. 'Ought to take us two, maybe three, hours. I'd say Carrizozo isn't more than half that far, so you ought to be there in half the time. When you get there, find the sheriff. Tell him what we've done and why. Tell him to get some men out here to fix that rail, and tell him to get word to the U.S. marshal in Santa Fe.'

'You betcha,' Pat Seele said. 'Come on, Moses!'

'One other thing,' Leaven added. 'Tell him we're going to try going over Bonito Lake and then down toward the Ruidoso. He may want to cut east through Capitan an' head us off.'

'I'll tell him,' Seele promised, and something like two and a half hours later, footsore, weary, and parched, he sat in the blessed, dark coolness of the sheriff's office in the Carrizozo Court House.

Sheriff George Curtis was a slat-thin, cadaverous-looking man of about thirty. He wore his gun like a farmer, high on his belt, and fastened to it with a thong looped around the spur hammer of the .45. His bucolic appearance had misled a number of would-be badmen, for Curtis was neither stupid nor slow; there weren't more than a dozen men in the county who could shoot as well as he could — perhaps only two could shoot better. George Curtis was also phlegmatically deliberate. He listened very carefully to what Pat Seele told him, then carefully checked what Seele had told him with the stoker — with a natural courtesy that took no regard of the color of Moses' skin. From there he got a picture of the three raiders and a fairly concise idea of the two Pinkerton men as well. Satisfied that the Pinks wouldn't cause him more trouble than the fugitives by getting themselves lost in one of the thousands of box canyons striating the western slopes of the White Mountains, he went out and got his posse together.

Sheriff Curtis' posse wasn't what you might have expected. There were none of the swaggering buck-skin-clad *pistoleros*, who had been common in Lincoln County not many years before. It had no imported toughs from Seven Rivers or the Texas Panhandle, who could do things with brands that had to be seen to be believed and who could also, when necessary, turn their skillful hands to cold-blooded murder, arson, or rape. There were no hawk-eyed Apache trackers who could follow birds through the air or fish through the water. A man didn't need any of that dime-novel stuff in this part of the country.

Curtis rousted out old Nicky Cantilles, seventy years old if he was a day, an old Spanish-American settler from 'way on back when the stoutest building in the county had been the

Torreon in Lincoln, or *Placita* as they'd called it then. Old Nick was built of whang leather and chewing tobacco, and he could still fork a mountain mule for longer than most youngsters could ride in a wagon. He also knew every inch of every draw, every runoff, and every canyon between White Oaks and the Tularosa and clear off the way across to South Spring on the Pecos.

The second member of Curtis' posse was a half-breed Mescalero named Jim-Bob Panther. And there was a very sound reason for having Jim-Bob along — he was a kind of insurance policy. If they ran into any Mescaleros there in the deeper recesses of the forests that clad the rolling hills of the reservation, like as not there wouldn't be any trouble. But if the Apaches had happened on some money and used that money to buy liquor at Murphy's old brewery above the fort or at Dowlin's, they'd like as not slit the throat of any white-eye they came across for the coins in his pocket or the clothes on his back. Also, Jim-Bob was no mean shakes as a tracker, given half a break. From what Seele had told him the Pinkerton men said, Sheriff Curtis didn't reckon to get many of those.

Finally, he rousted out his own deputy, Tony Coyle. Tony was a lazy-looking farmer's son, long-legged and sleepy-eyed, but he could shoot the eye out of a quail in flight.

'Well, Nick,' Curtis asked the old man. 'That's the picture. What you reckon?'

'I reckon any man's a damn fool rides all the hellangone across the White Mountains an' down to the Pecos to git to Santy Fe,' Cantilles told him. 'But I reckon them eastern dudes might be half-right, at that.'

'Given they've turned east, not headed up north,' Curtis said, 'which way you reckon they might head?'

'Ain't all that many options, y'ask me,' Tony Coyle drawled.

He was right. There weren't. You could head uphill into the Little Cub

Mountains — not mountains at all, really, but pretty big for hills. There was a pass of sorts between Nogal Peak and Church Mountain, after which you could pick up Nogal Canyon and come down alongside the lake and then swing north toward Capitan. But that was hard going for horses. Mules could do it. Nick Cantilles discarded as unlikely the trail through Nogal Canyon.

'How about cutting back off Spring Canyon and down into Turkey Canyon?' Curtis asked. 'There's a trail around Bonito Lake that leads down to the main trail between Capitan and Ruidoso. Or we could pick up the old logging road.'

'I know the one,' Nick Cantilles snapped, as though his professional reputation had been challenged. 'Goes up through the hills to Fort Stanton. I'da thought them old boys was keen to stay away from anyplace they was soldiers.'

'Yeah, you're right,' Curtis admitted.

'They could cut south,' Tony Coyle said.

'South? South?' Nick snapped. 'What d'ye mean, south?'

'That ol' loggin' road you's talkin' 'bout,' Coyle answered. 'Turns south just a coupla miles short o' Fort Stanton.'

'Right, b'God!' wheezed Nick, as though exasperated and pleased at the same time. 'Damn near forgot! Goes right on down Eagle Crick an' brings you out on the Ruidoso just above San Pat!'

San Patricio was a huddle of Mexican adobes, most of them owned or part-owned by the Sedillo family, which stood on the Rio Ruidoso — the Noisy River — a mile or two above its confluence with the Bonito, where they both became the Hondo.

'And from San Pat,' Curtis mused. 'Nothin' but a barbed wire fence between there and the Arctic Circle!'

'Sounds like a good bet to me — if'n your train-robbers know this country,' Coyle said, getting to his feet.

'They know it,' Curtis said, with a

certainty in his voice he could not have justified if asked.

He led them out of the room, leaving Pat Seele and Moses Glorification Washington to their own devices. They limped to the door to see the sheriff swing into the saddle and whirl his horse around onto the trail leading due east into the hills.

'Hey! Sheriff!' Seele shouted. 'What about us?'

Curtis frowned, his expression that of a man reminded of his manners.

'Oh, sorry!' he shouted. 'Damn near forgot! Thanks!'

He was gone in a boiling cloud of dust, with Coyle and the old Mexican on his heels. The sheriff thundered off up the trail toward Capitan, and Pat Seele took off his engineer's cap and slammed it to the ground with a curse that could have broken windows.

4

The three train-robbers knew the country, all right. They had gotten to know it very well while they'd been riding with the Seven Rivers boys during the 'troubles' — what people were now starting to call the Lincoln County War. A stupid name, as though those latest troubles were isolated and a once-only thing. Shee-heet, man, there'd been wars of one kind or another in Lincoln County since the day it was set up, and it had been men like Pete Hainin, Dick Briggs, and Jim Lawrence who'd done the dirtiest fighting in them.

Those had been good days, well-paid days, days when you could pick up a few dozen of old Uncle John Chisum's steers and haze them over the hills to Lincoln, blotting their brands along the way. The 'House' would always see you right, either with cash or (more likely) credit at the store. You could play pool or billiards there with the army officers over from Stanton, play cards in the Masonic Rooms, or drink in the bar below. There was *bailes*, Mexican dances, where you could always find a plump little senorita to swing around and maybe meet in the darkness later.

But that had all changed after the big fight up in Lincoln the preceding July. They'd burned out the lawyer and the dregs that were left of the Regulators and taken everything that wasn't nailed down out of the Englishman's store. But that was the end of the pickings. Most of the 'boys' had taken advantage of the governor's amnesty, but not these three. These three were professionals, and they wanted no man's charity. So when they'd been approached to pull the holdup of the Southern Pacific and told there was twenty thousand in it for each of them, they had needed no second invitation.

Yes, they knew the country, and they

knew how to get lost in it.

Yes, they knew how to take orders.

Yes, they knew how to throw dust in any pursuer's eyes.

Three of them.

Hainin, the leader, was a tall, well-built man in his thirties. Hatless, his long hair curling well below the open collar of his woolen shirt, his drooping mustache concealed a mouth that looked like a wound. His faded blue eyes were constantly on the move, scanning the open country around them as they rode.

'Take it easy, Pete,' the man beside him said softly. 'Relax. You're wound up like a trod-on side-winder.'

Dick Briggs was a head shorter than Hainin, and everything about him looked blunted — short arms, stubby-fingered hands, and a bullet head with a flattened, fighter's nose. But his shoulders were sloped and powerful, his eyes beneath protruding brows not so much shrewd as foxy. He had tightly curled dark blond hair cut very short, so that pink scalp showed through on top.

'I'll relax when we're spendin' our winnings,' Hainin said. 'You keep your eyes skinned as well, Dick.'

Briggs nodded, though there wasn't much to keep your eyes occupied. They'd come up through the White Mountains just about the way that Sheriff Curtis and old Nick Cantilles had figured they would, the way men who knew enough about the country and how steep a hill their horses could climb would come. They had climbed up the slanting steep track along the southern slope of the canyon, at the bottom of which the Rio Bonito — the Pretty River — trickled and died, submerging beneath swathes of bleaching sand or burrowing beneath huge snow-shifted boulders. Its cutbank edges were a sharp brown against the dullness of the surrounding countryside. The Bonito ran off northeast toward Lincoln, but the three men crossed the divide, moving southeast, and were edging down onto the logging track — hardly more than rutted scars torn into the spongy, springy grass by the Mescaleros who came up there to fell trees for old Dowlin on the Ruidoso or Blazer up near the Indian agency. It looped between the sage-stuccoed shoulders of two long low hills that fell away into shallow canyons north and south. They were riding along a flat hogback, fairly high up, toward the curve in the logging track that would lead them down in snaking curves to Eagle Creek, which they would then follow south toward the Ruidoso Valley.

Briggs glanced back at the third member of the party. 'How you comin', Jamesie?' he asked.

'Fine as snakehair,' Lawrence answered.

'You take care o' that nag o' yours,' Briggs said. 'He's worth his weight in gold!'

Jim Lawrence grinned. What Briggs said wasn't far short of the truth. They had taken time out along the way to burst open the slatted crate holding the money and to pack the wadded bundles into two big *alforjas*, which were now slung across the cantle of Lawrence's saddle.

Lawrence was about to say something when he heard Hainin shout. Looking up, he saw three horsemen swing into view around the bend in the logging trail ahead. He cursed in startled panic. Who were they? What the hell — ? He didn't have to formulate the question. The lead rider in the trio ahead reached down and hoisted a carbine out of the saddle holster under his right leg. The gun metal caught sunlight as the man swung the gun up and kicked his horse into a run, but the three raiders were already on the move. Long before they had come to this place, they had discussed what they would do if pursued, if the law got on their trail. They had discussed it not two hours before, when they were repacking the bundles of money, only half-joking about any one of them getting away and taking off with the whole haul — and about the other two being as certain as Sunday to track down the one who'd run with the money and kill him like a bug. They had made their plans, set their rendezvous, and planned their routes for just such an eventuality.

'Scatter!' Hainin yelled. 'Get the hell out of here!'

There was little or no cover right or left. On the left the ground rose steeply, and greasewood and sage tangled with briars, bramble, and scree underfoot — difficult ground for any horse to cover fast. Hainin rocketed off to the right, digging in his spurs until blood spurted from the horse's side and the animal was galloping flat out with head stretched low, ears back, and eyes rolling wildly. He steered the horse straight for the sloping brow that sharpened into a sliding shale runoff and went down steeply to the canyon floor below, where the timber was dark and thicker.

Briggs took the left-hand side but quartered back across to a spot where a shale runoff gave his laboring horse a halfway decent chance of making it to the crest before any pursuer could duplicate his running rush at the slope. Lashing his horse like a man demented, the reins raising welts on the chestnut's withers, Briggs galloped up the bare, rocky hillside while Jim Lawrence, without hesitation, reined his own horse around and tore downhill. The horse went down the uncertain ground too fast to be able to see where he was putting his feet, and Lawrence had all he could do to stay on the back of the kicking, flailing animal. They went down into the Bonito Canyon like a bat out of hell, much too erratic a target for anyone above to hit and much too recklessly for anyone to follow the same path. Even as he fought the animal upright, sliding it on its haunches down a broken cutbank, Lawrence was figuring his route. He'd have to get across to South Fork and turn north toward Capitan, then cut through Capitan Pass on to the old military road that went down toward Chisum's and the open, sloping plains on the eastern edge of the endless mountains. Taking that route, a good rider could make enough ground to lose any pursuer.

Behind him Lawrence thought he heard shots. Maybe a Winchester; he couldn't be sure because of the wind in his ears. He wondered whether Hainin and Briggs had gotten away.

Not that it made any difference. They'd been told the job was worth sixty thousand. If three of them turned up to collect, that was twenty each. If only two, thirty each. The slope leveled out, and he patted the horse's neck, moving him at a canter toward the gap in the trees that led to the South Fork crossing.

Briggs wasn't anything like as lucky. His horse panicked, shying and bucking, unable to master the sliding shale that moved every time it got its hoofs set. Briggs panicked even more than his steed, and he screamed at it, larruping

44

the unfortunate beast with the long reins, which only increased its fright. The horse buck-jumped one more time and then stopped with its head down, lungs bellowing. In that moment Tony Coyle shot the beast out from between Briggs's legs. Briggs's horse went down in a floundering welter of legs and thrashing head, and Briggs was thrown, bundled and awkward, against a sharp-edged rock that caught him below the center of the spine, numbing his legs as he fell. He rolled down the shale slope, face and hands ripped by the chattering slate he dislodged, tumbling into a heavy thicket of greasewood that stopped him sharp, breaking his fall. Slightly bruised and shaken, Briggs was still fast and good, and he was halfway to his knees drawing his six-gun out of his holster when he saw the bony, high cheekboned face of Sheriff Curtis and then the Cavalry model Colt .45 leveled unwaveringly at his belly.

'Don't you go and do anythin' fatal, now,' Curtis advised him.

5

'Well,' the attorney general said, 'we've got one of them.'

'But that's all we've got,' Wells added.

They were sitting in the attorney general's office on the first floor of the Justice Department headquarters; Wells in the same leather chair he usually occupied, the attorney general leaning forward across his desk. The second armchair was occupied by a third man, younger than both the others, broad-shouldered and rangy, the kind of man you knew would be very tall when he stood, no matter how he might scrunch down into an armchair. His dark gray suit was well-tailored, but he seemed constrained by it, as though he might prefer something much more practical and comfortable. His face was tanned, the cheekbones not quite high enough to hint at mixed blood but giving his

46

face a flat, planed look, which together with level gray eyes, sun-bleached hair, and the tapering hands and fingers of an artist, made him look like some kind of an executive for a company whose business was mostly out of doors. And in a manner of speaking, that was what he was. His name was Frank Angel, and he was a special investigator: Angus Wells's discovery and his top trouble-shooter.

Wells knew what others did not know about Frank Angel. He knew about the bullet scars in both of Angel's legs and the longer one in his belly, and he knew how they had gotten there. He knew that if you checked Angel's hands more carefully, you would find the outer edges calloused, for the man was well trained in the martial arts of the Orient. He knew that if you put any kind of gun into Angel's hands, Angel could kill with it; and he knew the other things you could not see about Angel — the concealed throwing knives he could use so unerringly, the razor-edged buckle clipped behind the ornate one he usually wore, the peg-ended wire garotte looped inside the wide leather belt. He knew all about Frank Angel because he had taught Angel a great deal of it and had been there to see that Angel had been taught all the rest. He also knew that he owed Angel his life, but neither of them had ever spoken of that.

'Goddamn it, they can't have just vanished off the face of the earth!' the attorney general said. 'Two men with a quarter of a million dollars don't just disappear!'

'I don't know,' Wells mused. 'I'd have said that with that kind of money, anyone could disappear. Buy a new name, a new country even.'

'In ten days? Hardly!' snorted the attorney general.

'Where's Briggs now?'

It was the first time Frank Angel had spoken since he'd come into the room. He'd listened to the theories. Wells had several. The old man had a few of his own. The robbers were lying low, waiting until pursuit died down before they spent their loot. Or they weren't and were papering one of the big cities with federal money, and nobody had even noticed. Or they had split up and were awaiting word from Briggs. Or they weren't. He shrugged mentally. Made no difference. Ten days had passed since they took Dick Briggs, and nothing else had turned up.

He'd read the reports. Engineer Pat Seele: Southern Pacific Railroad employee for eighteen years, married, four kids, living in a small frame house on the outskirts of Trinidad, Colorado. Exemplary record, unlikeliest of unlikely candidates to have been implicated in the robbery, unless you counted the Negro stoker with the magnificent name — Moses Glorification Washington. All they'd been able to say about the man who'd held them at gunpoint was that he was about five feet nine, had sallow skin and green eyes. At least, they thought they were green. The other two they'd seen only from a distance. One thickset and stocky, the other tall with long dark hair — not much more help than the descriptions given by the two Pinkerton men.

Sheriff George Curtis had also put in a report on the men he'd seen. The one riding a chestnut had been tall with long dark hair (he'd lost a hat in his flight, but the hat was old, sweatstained, and indistinguishable from a thousand other hats), and the other man had been so far away that he could only make out a dark blue shirt and pants and his excellent riding. Curtis had the feeling that the trio knew the area well, and it was possible that they'd been involved in the Lincoln troubles a year or two before. Which, Angel reflected, cut the number of possibilities down to seven or eight hundred.

The only positive lead was Briggs.

'He's in the territorial penitentiary at Folsom,' Wells replied. 'Why?'

'He's no use to us there,' Angel said.

'Take your point, Frank,' Wells said.

'But we can't risk losing him if we turn him loose. Even the best shagger in the business would run a fair chance of either being spotted and taken or dodged without too much trouble. And we don't know if his sidekicks aren't watching out for just such a dodge.'

'Hardly likely,' Angel suggested.

'Too chancey,' was the firm reply.

Angel just shrugged.

The attorney general reached for the box on the right-hand side of his desk and took out one of his evil-smelling cigars. He raised an eyebrow at the two men, who politely but firmly shook their heads in refusal. With a shrug that almost said that they were out of their heads, the attorney general lit his cigar with a wooden match, inhaling with deep pleasure. Wells looked at Frank Angel, and although their faces showed nothing, each knew what the other was thinking. They'd both, at one time or another, accepted the old man's offer — but only once. After choking politely for what seemed like interminable hours, both had vowed never to touch the cigars again under any circumstance. They privately agreed that the attorney general probably had the cigars manufactured in a South American banana republic by very fat, very sweaty peons who created the unique flavor and bouquet by using a mixture of horse manure and wet newspaper to roll the stogies and stored them in the outhouse of the town brothel to mature.

'Well Angus, Frank,' the attorney general said, puffing happily on the glowing cigar, his head wreathed in pungent smoke. 'Those Treasury boys want some answers, and they want them fast. We're in trouble if we don't come up with them.'

'There is a way,' Angel said.

Both men turned to look at him, and Angel grinned. When the old man said 'we' were in trouble, what he meant was 'you' were — and up to your eyebrows in it. If there was trouble, he wasn't in it. No way.

'Let's hear it,' the attorney general said. He sat down in his big leather chair, spreading his hands on the polished desk and looking expectantly at Frank Angel. Wells, too, eased himself into his chair, watching carefully, as though Angel were going to ask a conundrum he might have to answer.

'Frame me,' Angel said.

'What?'

'Rig a robbery, something fairly heavy. Something involving a lot of money — gold, perhaps. Something that might impress a man who can lay his hands on a one-third share of a quarter of a million dollars.'

'Yes,' Wells said. 'I'm with you. You get pulled in for this job, whatever it is. Thrown into the pen. But it won't get you anywhere.'

'Why not?' Angel asked.

'Briggs won't cough,' Wells told him. 'He's like a rock. I've had three men in there working on him. Tried every trick in the book. Told him we'd taken the other two, he might as well spill. He laughed in their faces. Told him the money had been recovered, his pals had run for it leaving him holding the baby. Not a peep. Either he really doesn't know anything, or he knows he's fireproof.'

'Which do you think it is?' Angel asked.

'Fireproof,' Wells answered.

'There's something else, though,' Angel put in thoughtfully. 'Something we could try.'

Wells leaned back in his chair, eyes narrowing slightly. He took a deep breath as the attorney general nodded for Angel to continue.

'Put me in with Briggs. Let me see if I can win his confidence. Three days at the most. If I do, I'll pass a signal. Then you fix it, Angus — fix it so we can escape, crash out.'

'Are you out of your head?' Wells said harshly. 'You think the territorial penitentiary will stand for having its reputation ruined?'

Angel looked at the attorney general,

who was frowning.

'The territorial penitentiary will do what it is damned well told to do, Angus,' the old man said, 'if I'm the one that tells it.'

'It's only a chance,' Angel said, 'but it might work.'

'You might also get your throat cut,' Wells pointed out. 'This Briggs might get on to you.'

'He might,' Angel admitted. 'It's worth trying, If we got together — as sidekicks — he might lead me to the others. Or the money. Or both.'

'I don't know,' Wells said. 'It's a damned long shot, Frank.'

'Name another we can try,' Angel said flatly.

There was a silence. If Wells had any other thoughts on the idea, he kept them to himself. The attorney general fell silent, too, tapping his teeth with a pen.

'Yes,' he said, finally, decisively. 'I think we'll try it.'

Angel didn't smile. He wasn't being

rewarded. It was just a good idea. It might work, and it might not. It depended on how good they could make the escape look and if he could swing Briggs' friendship. He said as much.

'Oh,' Wells said softly. 'I think we can make it look good, all right. That is, if you can break Briggs.'

'There'll be a way,' Angel said. 'There always is.'

'All right,' the attorney general said. 'That's it. Angus, I leave the details to you. Get on to it and make it look good. Frame Angel so he only just avoids being hung!'

He smiled to take the sting out of his words. 'Good luck, boy,' he said to Angel.

'Thanks,' Angel said. He figured he was going to need it.

6

There wasn't much you could say about the cells in Folsom. There wasn't a hell of a lot more you could say about the whole damned place. It sat like some kind of monstrous concrete fortress on a bluff just south of the Cimarron, where the road from Raton to Clayton bisected the monotony of the sage-stippled plain. The ground between the sloping walls and the river was bare and featureless, with hardly enough cover to protect the gophers from the wheeling hawks. To the south the Sierra Grande rose eight and a half thousand feet in the sky, dominating the mesas beneath it.

The prison itself was simple but not makeshift. A ten-foot-high wire fence separated the prison from a twenty-foot-wide no-man's-land, patrolled by armed guards. The outer walls were octagonal, and on every angled corner there was a guard post manned by two armed guards who had almost a 180-degree coverage of both the ground outside their stations and the exercise yards inside. The walls were made of huge square blocks of limestone quarried down south near Carlsbad and freighted up to this desolate corner of the territory by ox-teams. The prison buildings were gray and featureless, the windows tiny and barred. From the corners of the square central administration block, two stories high, radiated the cell blocks, each of them exactly the same except for an identifying letter: A, B, C or D. On each block were eight cells on a central corridor patrolled regularly by armed guards. In each cell were two prisoners.

Armed guards were stationed at the perimeter fence, and they checked everything carefully before opening the padlocked gate and letting the wagon through. The heavy steel-studded, metal-plated gates grated and squalled as they swung back, allowing the wagon carrying Angel, whose arms and legs were chained together, onto the grounds. Again the business with the documents. The closing gates, clanging behind with an awful finality, cut off the sunlight, and Angel shivered in a shadowed chill of the triangular, cobbled yard. He was helped out of the wagon none too gently, and they marched him across to yet another guarded gateway, the doors made of what looked like steel-reinforced oak. After his papers were checked, they were admitted into a concrete corridor; and escorted — again by armed guards — to the left. A right angle turn — Angel assumed from the light coming in from windows high above his head that the corridor was on the outside of the square administration building — and through another door. Beyond it were stone stairs rising in a wide half-circle. A corridor at the top, and then another solid oak door with metal straps and bolts reinforcing it.

They registered him, measured him, doused his hair with delousing powder, stripped him, and examined him medically. They confiscated all his clothes and issued him a shapeless tunic and pants of yellow and black hooped stripes, a soft forage cap, and boots without laces. He began to understand how prison depersonalizes men when they gave him a board with the number 4855, told him to hold the board in front of his chest, and the photographer took his picture, firing the flash powder with a fizzing *whoomphf* that made the guards flinch.

Then he was hurriedly marched down the stairs and through the sliding barred gates that led to Cell Block A.

'Number twelve for you, forty-eight-fifty-five!' the guard snapped.

'On yer right, hup-hi, look alive now!'

Sliding clang of steel door moving aside. Two cots. Stinking bucket in the corner. Formless shape on the right-hand cot ignoring his arrival. Whitewashed limestone walls dripping with condensation. A chilly dampness in the air.

And silence.

Tangible, a humming silence that told him he had been watched, measured, weighed, assessed by every prisoner in the block.

Heavy footsteps as the guards paced up and down the corridor.

No way to measure time.

'What you in for?'

Angel lay on his cot looking at the ceiling. He had seen Briggs get up off his cot and sized the man up without actually appearing to look at him. About five nine or ten, he figured. Hundred and eighty pounds or so — the build of a wrestler, a professional brawler. Bullet head with cropped dark blond hair, a flattened pug's nose. Sloping, powerful shoulders that even the shapeless convict's suit couldn't hide. Pale, almost green eyes beneath protruding eyebrows that gave the man's face a foxy, cunning look. He ignored the question.

'I said, what you in for?'

Angel sprang off the cot like a tiger. His forearm came across Briggs's throat like a bar of steel, and he smashed the man back against the seeping wall, causing Briggs's eyes to pop with fear that burned with surging anger. He could feel Briggs's mounting resistance; and with the knuckles of his right hand, he delivered a short, hurting blow that hardly seemed to have any power behind it. Briggs collapsed, his heart momentarily stunned by the driving force of Angel's hand, his mouth falling open as he gasped for oxygen.

'Uccchhh,' Briggs managed.

'Stay the hell away from me, you punk!' Angel rasped. He yanked Briggs around and thrust him away from him. Briggs's legs hit the edge of his cot, and he collapsed on it. He held up his hands in surrender, and Angel turned away. Then he stretched out on his cot and stared at the ceiling again, listening to Briggs gradually bring his breathing under control and fall silent. Neither man spoke again all day.

Food was brought to them after what Angel figured must have been five or six hours. Suppertime, he thought? Six, seven?

He got up and tipped the food into the slop bucket in the corner. Briggs watched him in astonishment, mouth full of food falling open.

'Hey,' he began, then shut his mouth quickly as Angel wheeled around threateningly to face him.

End of day one.

Bells clanging, clanging, clanging, woke Angel. He couldn't remember having fallen asleep. He was stiff and cold and uncomfortable. Briggs was moving about the cell, a grubby towel looped across his forearm, finally coming to a stop by the cell door with a bright, expectant look. There was a lot of movement in the corridor outside. Angel swung his feet down to the floor as the cell door was slid back. A burly, red-faced guard came in, swinging his billy.

'On your feet, you!' he snapped, flicking the club over. It rapped on the side of Angel's head, stunning him momentarily. He lurched to his feet, hands reaching automatically for the man, who took a skipping, trained step backward and hit him again with the club. Angel went down on his knees, still reaching for the guard, who blew his whistle. Briggs cowered in the corner of the cell by the open doorway. Two more guards came running in and saw Angel on his knees in the middle of the cell. They hauled him to his feet and dragged him out into the corridor. All the other prisoners were lined up there, and they watched impassively as Angel was dragged, feet trailing, the length of the cell block. The two guards dumped him into a stone trough of cold water at the end of the corridor, and when he recoiled, spluttering, trying to climb out, they jeered at him and pushed him in again with their feet. Drenched and choking from the fetid water he had swallowed, Angel was yanked out of the trough and dumped onto the floor. Before he could get up, one of the guards sank a boot into his ribs. He felt a sharp, sweet pain in his rib cage.

'Get your ass off the floor, pig!' shouted the burly guard who had first come into the cell. 'I'll let you off light because you're new here! No breakfast for you — just forty times around the yard with the log!'

There was a murmur from the watching prisoners. Nothing more, just a sibilant murmur stilled instantly by roared threats from the guards. They dragged Angel outside, one of them holding each arm, hustling him quickly along. Lying on the floor was a foot-thick log, perhaps three feet long, greasy with dirt and mold.

'Pick it up!' the guard snapped. 'On your shoulders! Smart now! Hup-hi!'

Angel grabbed the two metal cleats on the log and hoisted it onto his shoulders. They made him run around the exercise yard while the other prisoners watched. It wasn't more than fifty yards each time, but they made him carry the log until his shoulders were totally numb, his legs like molten rubber, and his back a solid mass of shooting pain so complete that he felt as if he were on another plane of existence. The guards watched his reeling figure from above as it staggered around the cobbled yard, falling, cursing, weeping, getting up, and staggering on, endlessly, endlessly, until finally they had had their sport with him and he was dragged back into the cell and thrown on the cot.

'Next time, on your feet sharp and ready for ablutions!' yelled the red-faced guard. 'Got me?'

Frank Angel tried to spit into the glaring face, thrust within feet of his own, but his mouth was bone dry and his lips bloody and cracked where he had bitten them. He tried to straighten out his back on the cot. The pain made him cry out loud. Eventually he lapsed into unconsciousness.

★ ★ ★

It was so black when he opened his eyes that he thought for one terrible moment he had gone blind. Then he realized that it was not the total, empty black of sightlessness but the ordinary darkness of night. Something had awakened him, and after a while he realized it was Briggs standing above him with a wet rag in his hand. He had bathed Angel's parched mouth with it and was about to do so again when Angel moved in the darkness. His hand grasped Briggs's throat, forcing the man backward. Briggs reacted quickly, and his strength was far greater than Angel's. He knocked Angel's hand away and pinned him down on the cot, breathing heavily. 'For Christ's sake, man, I'm tryin' to help you!' he hissed.

'Fuck you!' Angel gritted, trying — not very hard — to push Briggs off him. 'I don't want no help from you or nobody else!'

Briggs made an angry sound. With

the palm of his hand he slammed Angel back flat against the top of the cot. 'You'll last about ten minutes in this place, you carry on like that, friend!' he hissed. 'Keep your voice down or you'll have every guard in the damn place in here beatin' on your thick skull!'

Angel relaxed, lying back and showing Briggs that he was not resisting.

Briggs nodded. 'That's better,' he said. 'Here, wipe your face.' He handed Angel the rag, and half-warm though it was, it brought blessed relief to the bruises and cuts.

'What you tryin' to do, anyway?' Briggs asked. 'Take on the whole goddamn prison?'

'Motherfuckers!' Angel rasped. 'Pig screwin' sadists!'

'Uh-huh,' Briggs said. 'That'll get you a long way in here!'

'Shit,' Angel said. 'I won't be in here for long.'

'Sure,' Briggs said.

'You can bet on it,' Angel told him. 'I'm gettin' out, an' the first throat I'm cuttin' on the way is that bastard who worked me over!'

'You aim to talk him to death?' Briggs sneered.

'Not hardly,' Angel said, and showed him the knife.

End of day two.

*   *   *

'You could take me out with you,' Briggs said. 'I could help you.'

'Sure,' Angel said.

'You know this country?' Briggs asked.

'What difference does it make?'

'You wouldn't get five miles,' Briggs told him. 'If you had someone with you who knows the country . . . '

'Sure,' Angel said. 'Listen, Briggs, no offense. But amateurs just screw everything up.'

'Amateurs?' Briggs spat. 'What you talkin' about, amateurs?'

'You, Briggs. What you in for, anyway? Knockin' off a few head of cattle? Changin' someone's brand on a good horse? Shit, man, you're like the rest of these misfits in here — too dumb to steal anythin' big, too gutless to get into the big time.'

'Like you, huh?' Briggs retorted, stung by Angel's words. 'You're so A-OK like you say, how come you're slung into the pokey, big man?'

'Shit, you can't count poor luck,' Angel said. 'Poor luck don't count.'

'What you in for, then?'

'Tried to kill Tom Catron,' Frank Angel answered. 'You prob'ly don't even know who I'm talkin' about.'

Briggs looked at him with his mouth open. Thomas Benton Catron was probably the most powerful man in New Mexico, and rumor had it that most of the men who crossed his path from left to right tended to have a hell of a lot of bad luck afterward — real bad luck.

'You tried to *kill* Tom Catron?'

'Yeah. Just poor luck I didn't swing it The sonofabitch bent down to tie his shoe just as I cut loose. If I'd hit the trail right on afterward, no one'd ever've known. But I'm a pro, see. I tried for a second shot. An' they took me.'

'Christ, man,' Briggs said. 'How come they didn't hang you right there an' then?'

'Oh, I got a few friends o' my own. Catron might run most o' the politics around here, but he don't run all of them.'

'What the hell you want to shoot him for, anyways?' Briggs demanded.

'Money — what else?' Angel snapped. 'What the hell else?'

'Someone paid you to knock off Tom Catron?' whispered Briggs. 'Who?'

Angel looked at him with utmost contempt. 'Jesus H. Christ, you *are* dumb!' he said, shaking his head. 'No wonder you're rottin' in this pesthole. Well, rot away, Briggs. You're a nice guy, but you're not in my class. An' that's not vanity, either.'

'That's what you think,' Briggs said.

71

'Whatever it is, the hell with you, big shot!'

'All right,' Angel said wearily. 'Go ahead, convince me. You're a master-mind, right? What you did was to knock off some grocery store in a *placita* fifty miles from no place, huh? Or was it bigger than that? Maybe you got away with a couple o' hundred bucks from some drunken trail driver someplace or held up a county bank and made off with the life savings of three Mormon farmers. Boy, Briggs, I can't wait to hear it!'

'Me an' two other guys,' Briggs began, 'we . . . ' He hesitated and then fell silent, biting his lip. 'Forget it,' he said roughly. 'You just forget it.'

'Go on, big man,' Angel said roughly, pushing him now, knowing that if he didn't get Briggs to say it right now, he'd never say it at all. 'Tell me what you and these two other guys did that was so stupendous. I ain't had a good laugh since I come in here, anyway.'

'We knocked off a train,' Briggs said.

'With a quarter of a million dollars on board!'

Angel just looked at him. He didn't say a word, but the look on his face told Briggs what Angel was thinking.

'Goddamn it, it's true!' Briggs said, trying to keep the note of pleading out of his voice.

'Sure,' Angel said. 'I read all about it in the papers. Headlines a foot high. About how the train was robbed and all that money took. In a pig's eye! What you take me for, Briggs — some kind of idiot?'

'I'm tellin' you the truth,' Briggs said hotly. 'If it wasn't in the papers, it's 'cause they wanted to keep it hushed up. Figured maybe I'd crack, give them a lead to the others. Well, I never. Not a word.'

'That's some story,' Angel said. 'I'll give you that.'

'Goddamn it — ' Briggs started again, but Angel held up his hand.

'All right,' he said. 'Let's say I believe you.'

73

'You believe me?'

'Let's say I do.'

'Then let me make the break with you.'

'Why you want out, Briggs?'

'I want my share o' that robbery — what else?'

'Fine. What I mean is — why should I help you?'

'Jesus, we'd be helping each other, wouldn't we?'

'I'm the one with the knife,' Angel pointed out. 'I can get out o' here alone slick as snake oil. Why should I give you a hand? You got nothin' I need.'

'I got twenty thousand dollars waitin' for me outside,' Briggs said. 'You help me get out o' here, five thousand of it's yours.'

'I thought you said you got a quarter of a million?'

'Five thousand,' Briggs repeated, ignoring his question.

'Seventy-five hundred,' Angel said.

'Done,' Briggs replied. 'When do we go?'

'Tomorrow,' Angel said. 'Right after exercises.'

End of day three, and he had him.

Much, much later, he lay awake on his cot, thinking back over what Briggs had told him. There had been three of them; he knew that was the truth. Briggs hadn't lied about that nor the total amount taken from the train. So there was no reason to doubt that he had $20,000 waiting for him. But if his share was only $20,000, did that mean the other two were taking $115,000 each, and if so why?

He kept going back to his own theory about the robbery. He had contacted Larry James, a district attorney's man in San Francisco, and James did some discreet checking on the banks that had made up the shipment and on the personnel in those banks who had known about it. They all came up smelling of roses. The Pinkerton Detective Agency was happy to let someone from the Justice Department check out any of their people, and Angel personally looked over the dossiers of Leaven and Ruzzin. As far as he could tell, they were clean too, and when the bearded Mr Pinkerton told him that both men were checking their own back trail through Arizona and New Mexico, he was convinced of it. Pinkerton told him that Leaven and Ruzzin were as anxious to lay hands on the other two robbers as he was; if anything, more anxious, because the robbery reflected upon the Pinkerton Agency and by definition upon Leaven and Ruzzin personally.

Yet Angel felt strongly that the robbers were nothing more than that — especially if Briggs was a sample. Good men, cool, resourceful maybe. With local knowledge certainly. But not the kind of men who'd know about a shipment of that size, of that kind. Which led to another piece of the puzzle.

Suppose Briggs's $20,000 share was the same as that of the other two? A total of $60,000. Why would they accept so little when they had a quarter of a million in their hands — *unless they didn't know that the money couldn't be traced?* Which meant that they had been told it was. And that in turn meant that someone had told them about the shipment, how to take it, and where to take it. Planned every move of the whole robbery: only to be thwarted by Briggs's capture and Sheriff Curtis's pursuit. It had put the others to flight. Now they were hiding out, awaiting — what? Further instructions? Briggs knew. Briggs was the key.

These thoughts and many others twirled around and around in his head until finally he went to sleep. In his dreams a dark shape pursued him through mist. He could see where the mist ended and knew that when he reached that point someone would be waiting to kill him. He was not afraid of being killed. But he was afraid of finding out who was waiting. When he came to the place where the mist ended, he woke up. The bells were clanging, and it was morning.

7

The arrangements Angel had made through Wells with the warden of Folsom Penitentiary were simple to the point of imbecility. Since, as Angel had put it, he had no knowledge of the warden's intellectual powers, the best thing to do was avoid any chance of straining them. In actual fact, Warden Harry Abrams was a model penologist who loathed the conditions in which he had to keep his prisoners and was constantly campaigning through the Territorial Legislature, the Prison Board, and newspapers for funds with which to alleviate Folsom's problems. He was a short man, middle-aged, and running to florid fat as a result of the many formal lunches he had to attend or speak at. But he was shrewd and intelligent. He had listened to Wells carefully, made one or two pencil notes on a pad by his side, and nodded briskly when Wells had finished speaking. 'No problem with any of that,' he had said. 'How many others do you want let in on this?'

'The fewer the better,' Wells said. 'Let's work out the minimums.'

Abrams had been not only helpful but sensible. They had realized that Angel might receive same bad treatment (although neither man had any idea of exactly what the guards did to some of the prisoners, and since neither guards nor prisoners were likely to tell them, they had no way of preventing or changing it). But they decided against letting the guards in Cell Block A or in the main administration building in on the fact that the escape was rigged.

'It's got to look damned real,' Wells told him. 'Or Briggs will smell a rat.'

'I have to tell the guards in the wall sentinels,' Abrams told him. 'They're picked men, crack shots. They could pick both men off like flies from up there.'

'All right,' Wells said. 'But only the guards who are likely to see Angel — the others, no.'

That agreed, they settled down to more mundane details — clothes, horses, weapons.

'I don't think Briggs will wonder too much about the clothes and horses and guns,' Wells assured him. 'Angel will have told him about his powerful friends on the outside. He ought to swallow it. He's swallowed all the rest.'

Abrams nodded in agreement. 'I suppose so,' he said. 'Then all we have to do now is wait for Angel's signal.'

Wells nodded. The signal was a simple one. Angel would ask to see the warden before the exercise period. The request would be brought upstairs as a matter of course. The warden would deny the request. But he would know that Angel was ready, and Angel, when told the warden's decision, would know that the warden was.

So the request had been made and denied, and the wheels were in motion.

Angel hoped they were rolling smoothly while he and his fellow convicts were double-timed out of their cells and across to the dining hall, which with the kitchen took up the entire ground floor of the administration block. After breakfast the steel doors separating the four triangular yards were opened so that the prisoners could trot around the entire perimeter of the building — Warden Abrams's one concession against security, born of his feeling that prisoners should have, even in this most minimal of ways, a change of scenery at least once a day. There was little or no danger. On each of the sentinels in the eight corners of the octagonal wall, two sentries watched the shuffling prisoners with sharp eyes, ready for trouble, Winchester repeaters in their cradled hands. The heavy doors were locked, barred, and guarded. And all the way along the long crocodile of shuffling prisoners, every five or six yards, a prison guard marched, baton swinging, left hand on holstered pistol.

'Hup-hi, hup-hi, hup-hi!' the guards shouted their cadences, their breath a steamy fog in the chilly morning air. 'Hup-hi, hup-hi!'

As they came out of the yard between blocks A and D into the cobbled parade, which was dominated by big main doors, Frank Angel seemed to stumble and fell to the floor. In a moment, the big, red-faced guard from cell block A, whose name Angel now knew to be Chris Shore, was beside him, yanking brutally on his arm, the baton poised to strike.

'On yer feet, ye stumblebum!' Shore rasped.

He wasn't ready for the way Angel moved, wasn't anything like fast enough to stop the prisoner from coming up off the ground like a striking snake. His left hand moved from his right shoulder in a slicing chop that stopped with a slapping thud in the fold of flesh between Shore's chin and Adam's apple. A full strength blow would have destroyed his larynx, and Shore would have been dead in ten minutes. But Angel's blow merely paralyzed the guard's breathing. Shore's eyes bulged as his lungs tried desperately to draw oxygen through his stunned windpipe, and the baton clattered from a hand gone suddenly limp. Angel picked up the heavy club on the first bounce and as a second guard came running, threw it as if it were a balanced knife. The heavy, metal-covered billy whickered through the air. and the running guard ducked, flinching away. In a moment Angel was behind Shore, the knife in his hand flickering as it caught the first fleeting rays of the sun coming high enough to shine over the cray walls.

A running guard skidded to a halt, hand fumbling at the flap of his pistol holster.

'Touch that gun and you'll see his throat cut!' Angel yelled. 'Hear me!'

The guard looked about him wildly as the prisoners scattered to the safety of the outer walls, leaving the tableau posed in the center of the cobbled yard — Angel with his arm around Shore's neck, the fat man's spine arched back; the guard standing, hand poised over his holster, looking about him; the other guards frozen, waiting a moment. Briggs was about four yards to one side and edging forward. Angel wrestled Shore's gun out of its holster and tossed it to Briggs.

'Get over here close!' he shouted. 'Bring that guard here!'

Briggs gestured with the pistol, moving fast to be close to Angel and Shore. The other guard hesitated and Briggs fired the gun. The bullet smashed into the cobbles at the guard's feet, and he jumped visibly as the slug ricocheted away into infinity. Some of the prisoners near the wall ducked instinctively. The guard came warily forward, and then Briggs grabbed him. Now Angel swung Shore around in front of him for protection so that he was behind the fat guard and Briggs was behind Shore, dragging the other guard backward with the pistol against his temple.

'Open those gates!' Angel shouted. 'Open them up, or there'll be two dead guards out here!'

'Kill the guards and you'll be dead two seconds later!' one of the guards up on the prison wall yelled back. 'Turn them loose and give yourselves up!'

Briggs threw a shot toward the voice, and the guard ducked hastily back. The shuffling quartet edged nearer to the gates, and Angel shouted his order again.

'Open up,' he yelled. 'I won't say it three times!'

Warden Abrams was coming out of the main administration building now, flanked by three guards armed with sawed-off shotguns. They were ten gauge, riot guns, Briggs saw. If one of those was fired within twenty feet of a man, the remains usually had to be buried in a sandbag to give a decent weight to the coffin.

'Angel?' he said nervously.

'Keep cool,' Angel gritted. He dragged Shore, whose eyes were bulging with fear that drenched his face and body with perspiration, nearer to the gates.

'All right!' the warden shouted. 'We'll open up!'

A muttering cheer rose from the prisoners against the walls, and a dozen or so of them started forward toward Angel. Almost immediately a wicked volley of shots rang out from the sentinels around the walls, the bullets banging with ugly flat sounds into the cobblestones two feet in front of the moving prisoners.

The prisoners shrank back quickly as the warden shouted, 'Any man who tries to make a run for it will be shot down!' He walked out into the middle of the courtyard.

'You!' he called. 'You two men! If I open the gates, will you turn the guards loose unharmed?'

'Open the gates first, Warden!' Angel shouted. 'Or we'll kill them now!'

Warden Abrams nodded, waving his

arm in a signal to the men in the twin towers above the heavy gates. They worked the winches, and the doors slowly began to open. The guards on the perimeter fence came forward, their Winchesters cocked and ready.

'Hold your fire!' the warden shouted at them. 'Hold your fire!'

'All right, pig!' Angel hissed at Shore. 'Move ass!'

He thrust a knee into the fat man's back. Shore grunted in pain, walking as best he could with his back bent and Angel's arm like a bar of steel around his throat. Briggs dragged the other guard by the belt, moving the man awkwardly, but without risk. His pistol was jammed into the man's spine, and the guard knew that no matter what he might be able to do or not do to prevent or hamper the escape, it would result in his spine being blown to bits. The Territorial Prison Board didn't pay him enough to be that kind of hero.

'Get back away from me!' Angel rasped at the bayed guards near the gate. 'Inside, inside. Move yourselves!'

They saw the knife at Shore's throat, the pistol thrust into Angel's belt, and Briggs with his gun lammed into the other guard's back, They looked at the warden, who shook his head, and then, reluctantly, they edged away, backing off, sidling into the prison courtyard as the escaping men moved out into the no-man's-land between the walls and the perimeter fence, its gate now unguarded.

'All right, Warden!' Angel yelled. His voice sounded thin and unnatural in the open space after days of echoing against the walls of the cell. 'Shut the gates!'

'What about my men?' Abrams shouted back.

'Shut the gates, Warden!' Angel shouted. 'And be damned quick!'

Again Abrams gave a signal, and the men in the watchtower worked the winch that closed the gates. Abrams dashed across the yard, running up the stone stairs to the tower, his riot-gun-armed guards close behind him. The other prison guards were already in motion, hustling the prisoners back into the yard between cell blocks A and D, slamming the high metal barriers shut, sliding the bolts on the far side. The prisoners were herded into ranks — rebellious, muttering ranks, to be sure; but the glowering threat of the guards, all of whom had pistols drawn and were waiting for any overt movement, was enough to keep them quiescent.

'Turn those men loose,' the warden shouted. 'You haven't got a chance of getting away!'

'Up yours, you mealy-mouthed bastard!' Briggs shouted, and without warning aimed the pistol and threw a shot at the unprotected warden, The bullet was not carefully aimed, but Abrams was smacked backward as it ploughed a painful furrow through the muscle between his neck and shoulder. He cannoned into one of his guards, blood spurting over his light gray suit, and slid groaning to the floor.

'Goddamn you, for a stupid bastard!' Angel snarled at Briggs. 'What the hell did you do that for?'

'Ah, he was — '

'Shut your mouth and move!' Angel snapped. 'Get the hell out of range of those riot guns, at least. If we so much as show a finger now, one of those sons up there will shoot it off!'

They were finally outside the perimeter fence. Thirty feet from the walls. Now they hustled the two men, frog-marching them across the hilly ground as fast as they could go. Inside the prison a strident clangor began and rose to a crescendo as the alarm bells were set off. They could see guards with carbines in their hands running all along the perimeter wall.

Groaning, panting, cursing, slipping, and sweating, the two prisoners pushed and hurried the guards across the open ground away from the prison until they came to the wide, dusty road going south-east toward Clayton. On its far side was a sloping runoff, and they slid gratefully down into it, momentarily out of sight of the prison.

'All right,' Angel said, panting for breath. 'All right!'

Shore looked at him. He must have seen something in Angel's face that Angel could not conceal — a contempt, perhaps, that the guard read as decision.

'Oh, God,' Shore blubbered. 'Don't kill us, don't, don't, don't!'

'I sure as hell — ' Briggs said, cocking his pistol.

'Briggs!' Angel snapped at him, pushing the barrel of the revolver up and shoving the man away from his intended victim. Briggs growled angrily and brought the gun around on Angel.

'Keep off me,' he snarled. 'Keep your hands off me, or I'll kill you!'

'Go ahead,' Angel told him. 'How far you think you'll get alone? A mile? Two? They'll have you back inside there — ' he jerked his head back at the prison ' — so fast it'll singe your ass! Don't be a fool. They'll be coming out after us as

91

soon as they see these two, so we'd better make all the ground we can. You!'

Ignoring Briggs, he turned to face Shore, who flinched as though Angel had struck him. 'Yessir?' the guard managed.

'Take off your boots and your pants. Both of you!'

Shore began hastily to comply with Angel's order; the second guard hesitated until Briggs again cocked the revolver ostentatiously, whereupon he began to follow suit. In a few moments the guards stood, looking vaguely comic, in bare feet and grubby long johns. Angel took their boots and pants and tied them into a makeshift bundle.

'They can't walk five yards in any direction like that,' he grinned. 'This country's crawlin' with rattlers.'

He watched Shore's greasy face pale as he spoke, and the sound of the man's gulp was as loud as a cork being pulled out of a bottle. The other guard looked at Angel and spat on the ground.

'You're a pretty venomous bastard yourself, ain't you!' he said. 'Puttin' men barefoot where there's pizen critters.'

'I don't know,' Angel said mildly. 'Might be any snake bites you, he'll be the one gets poisoned. I wish I had the time to wait an' find out, but I ain't. Squat!'

The two men crouched where Angel indicated, sheltered from anyone's view by the cutbank above them.

'You stay put,' he warned them. 'Don't forget I'll be able to see you much longer than you'll be able to see me.'

He jerked his head at Briggs. 'Come on,' he said. 'Let's get the hell out of here.' He set off purposefully on foot, quartering due south to where Sierra Grande towered sharp and clear against the skyline, a banner of cloud drifting across her summit. The ground was soft and the going heavy in the laceless prison boots as they moved through the screening greasewood.

'What was all that bullshit about snakes?' he panted. 'Ain't no snakes this high up, an' you know it.'

'Sure,' Angel grinned. 'Question is, do them guards know it?'

The other man grinned too, admiring the ruse. 'How long you think it'll hold 'em?'

Angel was about to reply when, back in the direction from which they had come, they heard the faint sounds of men shouting.

'Answer your question?' Angel asked, as Briggs mouthed a curse.

They ran on through the broken land for another quarter of a mile, Angel's eye questing right and left constantly.

'Listen,' Briggs panted. 'Angel, listen. We got to . . . get horses. Get clothes — we can't wear these things . . . spiders on a whitewashed wall!'

'Take it easy,' Angel said. 'It's been taken care of!'

'What?'

'It's been taken care of,' Angel said,

and Briggs didn't hear the words, 'I hope,' that Angel added beneath his breath.

The two men stumbled into an open clearing, on one side of which was a flat rock. There was a splash of white on the rock, a striated chalk mark that could only have been made by man.

'This is the place!' Angel said. He slapped Briggs's back. 'This is it!'

Briggs looked at him as if he had gone mad. The sounds of pursuit were growing louder behind them, and Angel was acting like a man who'd just been dealt a full house.

Angel grabbed his arm and pulled him around behind the rock. There was a low stand of greasewood there. Tethered to one of the bushes were two saddled horses. Across the saddles were shirts, pants, and boots. And gunbelts. Briggs ran over to them, touching them like a kid on Christmas morning.

'Jesus!' he said, wonderingly. 'Jesus, Angel!'

'We got about ten minutes to get out of here!' Angel snapped. 'Come on, Briggs!'

He hoped to God he had the timing right.

8

He'd told them to make it look good, and they did. Almost too damned good.

He and Briggs swung into the saddle and kicked the horses into a gallop just as the guards burst through the screening bushes into the clearing. Whacking away over the broken ground, Angel thought for a moment that he saw Angus Wells among the pursuers, but that wasn't possible. Then he put his body down low along his horse's neck and concentrated on getting the hell out of there.

Behind him and to one side at least a dozen guards opened up with their Winchesters, the slugs whickering past the fleeing horsemen, smashing branches off the greasewood bushes, tearing leaping spouts of darkened sandy earth from the ground around, beside, and ahead of them. Interspersed amid the rattling cracks of the carbines was the duller *gbbbooomff!* of the riot guns, which were about as effective at the kind of range they were now being used over as throwing snowballs would have been.

Racing flat out away from the firing, Angel felt something touch his upper left arm. It was like someone lightly slapping a child, not in anger so much as in mild playfulness. He reeled sideways in the saddle, bright blood staining his arm, a gritted curse escaping his tensed lips. Goddamn, he'd told them to make it look good, but this was taking it too far! Straightening slightly in the saddle, he swiveled his arm around to look at it. It was a clean, burned rip, and it had done little more than take off a couple of layers of skin. Fool for luck, he told himself. If that bullet had gone an inch to the right, he'd be nursing a shattered left arm, about as much use in the game he was planning to play as a wooden-legged clown. If it had gone six inches to the right . . .

Well, no use thinking about that, he told himself as he reined his horse around. They were traversing a rising bluff that crested and sloped away down to Carrizozo Creek. There was enough water for them to ride in it for a while, and Angel headed down, signaling Briggs to follow.

'Where we headin'?' Briggs shouted.

'Further downstream there's a ford,' Angel told him. 'The old Santa Fe Trail crosses this crick.'

'The Cimarron cutoff?'

'That's right. We can follow the trail right on over to Las Vegas.'

'What's in Las Vegas?'

'Two things,' Angel told him, as they moved the horses at a walk down to the edge of the creek. 'One, a lot o' people who don't know who we are, an' what's more, don't care. Two, a telegraph office.'

'Telegraph office?' Briggs frowned. 'What the hell you need a telegraph office for?'

'Let my people know it all went well,' Angel said. 'An' where I'm headin' next. They'll maybe want me . . . available.'

Briggs nodded. He was very conscious of the fact that he had allied himself with a professional killer, and one who, if the evidence of the last few hours was anything to go by, had pretty powerful connections.

'Where would you be headin' next?' he asked cautiously.

'Why, Briggs, that's entirely up to you,' Angel said, with a wide grin. 'You tell me where that money you're gonna pay me for springin' you is, an 'we'll go fetch it. You pay me my seventy-five hundred, an' from there on in, you're on your own. Right?'

'Well,' Briggs hesitated.

'Now Briggs,' Angel said, very gently. 'You wouldn't go back on our deal, would you?'

'Hell, no, Angel,' Briggs said. 'It's . . . well, it's a bit more complicated than that.'

'It better not be too complicated, man,' Angel said, just the faint edge of warning anger making itself heard in his voice. Briggs caught the tone and held up a hand.

'No,' he said. 'I told you, though. There's others involved?'

'You can tell me all about it later, when we make camp,' Angel told him. 'For now, let's concentrate on puttin' some miles between us an' that stinkin' prison!'

'You figger they'll put a posse out after us, Angel?'

'Ain't figgerin' nothin',' Angel answered. 'Nor hangin' around waitin' to find out. Let's go, Briggs!'

He kicked his horse into a canter and splashed down into Carrizozo Creek.

★ ★ ★

'There was three of us,' Briggs began.

'You told me that,' Angel replied.

They had made a camp on the warm, southern side of a long sloping draw that ran slanting south-west toward the Canadian River. There was jerky and a flat bottle of whiskey in one of the *alforjas* slung behind the saddle and two cans of beans in the other. It wasn't Parisian cooking, but after the prison food it tasted like the purest nectar. Angel let Briggs drink most of the whiskey, contenting himself with a good slug to keep out the chill of the night. They foraged for enough wood to make a small fire in a sandpit, Apache style.

When the food was gone, Angel leaned back and invited Briggs to tell him the whole story. 'Who told you about the shipment?' he asked.

'Uh . . . listen, Angel, how'd you know about that?' Briggs asked, peering at him suspiciously in the fire-light.

'Shit, Briggs,' Angel said. 'You ain't the type'd know things like that. I'm figurin' your sidekicks didn't either.'

'No, they didn't,' Briggs muttered. 'You're right. Pete an' Jamesie, they're like me. Y'know — hired hands. He wanted good men who knew the country.'

'He?'

'The feller in Santa Fe. The one come to us with the proposition.'

'Oh,' Angel said, feigning only mild interest. *The name, the name*; he willed Briggs to say it.

'Got talkin' to him on the veranda outside La Fonda. You know it?' Angel nodded. Most of the business done among the Anglos — and not a few of the Spanish-Americans — who lived in Santa Fe was done over a drink after dinner on the porch of the rambling old hacienda which had become the capital's largest hotel. Most nights, you could go there and meet a man with sheep, cattle, or land to sell, find a man who wanted to buy any or all, and team up with someone who wanted company on a trip north, south, east, or west. Just as the Indian women sold their blankets and silver jewelry beneath the cool arches of the Palace of the Governors, so did the businessmen sell theirs on the lamplit La Fonda veranda.

'We adjourned somewhere more private. Some cantina down on the Alameda,' Briggs went on. 'Said he was lookin' for three or four men to do a dangerous job. They had to know the Tularosa country like the back of their own hands, he said. But if they did what he told them, they could make twenty thousand dollars each, clear. Shit, Angel,' he added, 'he might as well of said a million. Twenty grand is big money.'

'Right,' Angel said. *The name, man, the name*.

'Anyways, he sort of flamboozled around the subject for a while, an' then told us he'd like to ask around. Wanted to check on us, I reckoned. Pete reckoned the same. So we figured we'd check on him same time.'

'Pete?'

'Pete Hainin — him an' me an' Jamesie Lawrence pulled the job, remember?'

'You never told me their second

names,' Angel said.

'Oh,' Briggs said. 'Thought I did. Well, anyhow . . . ' He took another sizable gulp out of the almost-empty bottle, then held it up in the firelight, squinting ruefully at the level of the whiskey.

'Shit, I'm plumb sorry,' he said. 'Here, you — '

'No, finish it,' Angel said.

'Right,' Briggs said. He nodded wisely.

'You figured you'd check on the dude,' Angel reminded him,

'Oh. Yeah. Well, we couldn't find nothin' out about him. We asked all around town, only nobody'd ever heard of him.'

'What was his name?' Angel asked, idly.

'Never found that out, neither,' Briggs said. 'Asked him, next night when he looked us up in the *cantina*. Said we didn't need to know that.'

'But you knew he was from the East.'

'Hell, yeah. You ever see a westerner

wearin' flat-heeled boots?'

He made it sound like a sexual abnormality, and Angel grinned. Briggs ought to try tramping around the concrete pavements of New York for a few hours in the high-heeled riding boots he was wearing now. After an hour of it, he'd feel as if his spine was about three inches shorter.

'What was he, a big feller?'

'Big enough,' Briggs said. 'We never see him in really good light, you know? He allus sat in dark corners. In the cantina he allus had his hat down over his face. Allus made us leave after he did.'

'So he told you about the shipment,' Angel encouraged him.

'Right. Knowed all about it. Where the money was, how many men on the train. Told us exactly where we had to pull the job, how to do it. Told us the route we had to take over the White Mountains and up to Santa Fe. If we was chased, we was to split up. If we split up, we had three days to get to old

106

Fort Sumner, Beaver Smith's saloon. If it looked like any one of us had been taken, the other two was to move on, nice an' quiet. Stash the money away until it cooled, he said.'

'He told you the money was hot?'

'Right. He said we'd have to hide it away for a couple of months. Then we'd get our cut.'

'Where?'

'Said it didn't matter. He'd know where we were, and so he'd always be able to find the money.'

'Wasn't he scared you'd take off with the whole bundle?'

'Didn't act like it, I'll tell you that. He said if we crossed him, he'd spend the rest of his life huntin' us down, an' makin' sure all of us rotted in jail the rest of our days.'

'An' you believed that?'

'Sure, we did. Why the hell not? He was the kind you believe, and you can tie to that! Besides, we was happy enough to be gettin' a crack at twenty thousand each.'

'But you don't have it,' Angel said.

'No, but I ain't afeared,' Briggs said. 'Pete an' Jamesie wouldn't double-deal on me.'

'Beautiful,' Angel told him. 'All you got to do now is find them. And the money,'

'Hell, that's not gonna be so hard,' Briggs said. 'I figger I know where Jamesie'll be. An' he'll know where Pete is.'

'Pete's got the money?'

'He had it when I was took,' Briggs answered. 'Don't worry, he'll keep it safe.'

'Briggs,' Angel said flatly. 'You're a fool.' Briggs looked up quickly, bewildered at Angel's harsh words. 'What?' he asked. 'What?'

'Ain't it occurred to you that your dude is prob'ly lookin' for that money, too?'

'Well . . . hell, Angel, what you gettin' at?'

'Just this,' Angel told him. 'If the feller that hired you to pull that job can get to Lawrence and then to Hainin, he's only got to kill both o' them, an' he's free as a bird with the whole bundle in his pockets. What would you do — take him to court an' sue him for it?'

Briggs just sat there and looked at Angel, his mouth open. Angel watched the wheels turn in Briggs's head as the raider figured and added in his fuddled brain the implications of what Angel had just said. No matter which way he tried it, it came out looking like he might end up with a handful of nothing for robbing the Southern Pacific, for being on the wrong end of a territory-wide manhunt, and for the likelihood of a life sentence in Folsom if he was taken. Hainin, Jamesie, Lawrence, they were clean. Nobody knew about them.

'Jesus H. Christ, Angel,' he said, clambering to his feet in panic. 'Do somethin'! Contact them big mucky-muck friends o' yours an' get 'em lookin' for Pete an' Jamesie! We got to find them quick, afore that bastard dude does!'

'Saddle up,' Angel told him. 'We ride all night, we can be in Las Vegas before the telegraph office opens.'

9

They'd known right from the start that Angel wouldn't be able to get word direct to Washington. Not with Briggs breathing over his shoulder while he wrote his message in a telegraph office. So they'd decided on a very simple code which Angel could do in his head, without appearing to work it out, without needing a decoding log to set it up. All you had to do was to use the letter of the alphabet next to the actual one — so 'Angel' would read BOHFM.

'What the hell is all that?' Briggs asked wonderingly, as Angel printed slowly on the telegraph form.

'Code,' Angel said truthfully.

'The address, too?'

'Sure,' Angel said. 'My people are mighty careful about who reads their mail.' He tapped the side of his nose and looked mysterious.

'Uh-huh,' Briggs said. 'What's it say?'

'Says I got something needs doin', an' I want some walkin' money and good horses waitin' in Santa Fe. They can take it out of my account, I say. If they know anythin' about the present whereabouts of Pete Hainin or Jamesie Lawrence, to leave word.'

'That's great, Angel,' Briggs said. 'Listen, we get our mitts on that money, you're on a bonus. Ten grand each, OK?'

'That's big o' you, Dick,' Angel said, putting a warmth into his voice that he was far from feeling. 'OK, Jack,' he said to the telegrapher. 'Can you get this off right away?'

'Sure thing, mister,' the clerk said. 'What kind o' gobbledygook is this, anyway?'

'It's the kind that keeps telegrapher's clerks from readin' private messages,' Angel answered him coldly. 'What do I owe you?'

'Dollar ninety,' the clerk said, and when Angel told him to keep the change, he tossed the small coins onto the counter with a sneer.

'No thanks,' he said. 'I got too many private messages to read.'

He turned his back on the two men as they went out of the office and into the street where their horses stood. Watching impassively, he waited until they had moved off down the street toward the old town end, heading for the Glorieta road. When they were out of sight, he pulled down the blinds and scuttled out of the door, locking it behind him and trotting as fast as he could go up the Plaza Hotel in the square. Nodding to the desk clerk, he went up to the first floor and knocked on one of the doors. A voice told him to enter.

The big man sitting on the bed looked at him along the barrel of the leveled six-gun. Startled, the clerk recoiled, his hands moving involuntarily upward.

'Relax,' the man on the bed told him. 'Just cleaning it.'

There were no cleaning tools or oil or

rags anywhere, but the telegraph clerk decided not to mention it.

'He . . . them fellers came in, just like you said,' he told the man on the bed. 'They wanted me to send thisyere stuff out. Don't make no sense no how to me.'

'Don't let it worry you,' the big man said. He took the printed form and read it carefully, his lips moving as he figured out what it said:

HAVE BRIGGS CONFIDENCE STOP OTHERS INVOLVED PETE HAININ AND JAMES LAWRENCE STOP ALL THREE KNOWN STOP LINCOLN COUNTY SHOULD HAVE RECORDS SOME KIND HEADING VIA SANTA FE FOR RIO CHAMA COUNTRY WHERE LAWRENCE HAS WOMAN ON PLACE NEAR EL RITO STOP WHEREABOUTS HAININ WHEREABOUTS MONEY UNKNOWN AS YET STOP HAVE HORSES MONEY READY AT LA FONDA LEAVE WORD IF FIND ANYTHING USEFUL ABOUT HAININ OR

LAWRENCE NAME OF MAN WHO HIRED THEM ROB TRAIN UNKNOWN BUT BRIGG SAYS EASTERNER, SIX FEET OR OVER, WELL DRESSED, FLAT HEELED SHOES, BOSTON ACCENT.

The message was addressed to Post Box 34, Santa Fe. The man in the hotel room knew that Post Box 34 was the address of John T. Sherman, United States Marshal for the Territory of New Mexico. It would be Sherman's job to transmit the information in the telegraph back to the Department of Justice in Washington. He smiled, and without the clerk noticing, switched Angel's message for one he had written earlier. Handing this to the clerk, he flipped a twenty dollar gold piece out of his coat pocket toward the man, who caught it deftly. 'All right,' he said. 'Send it off.'

'Thanks, mister,' the clerk said, a twenty-dollar smile on his face. 'Thanks a lot!'

'Don't mention it,' the man said. 'And I want you to know that I mean just that: do not mention it.'

The clerk nodded, swallowing hastily. There was a look in the cold eyes of the man sitting on the bed that told him very, very clearly what would happen if he did mention it.

'Sure, sure thing, mister,' he said, backing out of the room.

The man watched him go with a thin smile and then picked up the Gladstone bag by the side of the drooping bed on which he'd spent the night with a Mexican whore. He slid the Frontier Model into a specially constructed pocket just forward of the hipbone on the left leg of his pants. The pocket was lined with leather and fitted with a strong spring at the bottom. The moment the hand touched the pistol butt, the spring clip was released, and the draw was rendered that fraction of a second faster. He had not had to use it yet; but the man who had made it for him was a master gunsmith, and he had no doubt that should the occasion arise, it would give him the edge he needed.

He paid his bill and hurried out across the plaza with its regimented shade oaks and ornate cast-iron bandstand, jostling heedless groups of indolent housewives gossiping in the shade. On the far side of the plaza, ready and waiting for him, was a buckboard with a fine span of thoroughbred bays. He had paid the youngster dozing in the driver's seat a peso to watch the team.

'*Vamos, compadrito!*' the big man said, slapping the youngster's leg. The kid jumped down, liquid eyes dancing, and watched as the big man popped the whip across the glossy haunches of the matched bays. They jumped into motion, moving around the square and down the long, wide main street toward the rutted ford across the river at the southern edge of town. It would take Briggs and Angel the better part of two days to get to Santa Fe: their horses were no longer fresh and had not been the best in the first place. By using the mountain cutoff, which took ten miles off the Glorieta route, and by pushing his horses to the limit, the big man knew he could be in the capitol in half that time. A day ahead of Angel the whole way. He smiled; not a smile of warmth and pleasure, but the smile of a cougar scenting its prey. A day would give him all the time he needed.

★   ★   ★

Briggs said he liked it up in the mountains.

You had to admit it was beautiful. Awe-inspiring, even. Way up above Espanola the trail was little more than a rutted track winding up into the mountains toward El Rito. The towering mountains on both sides of them thrust bald stone peaks up over the timberline. They had been steadily climbing most of the morning. The horses had been waiting, and there had been money in an unmarked envelope at the desk of the La Fonda. But nothing else. No word from Washington, nothing to warn Angel what might lie ahead. He had shrugged fatalistically. All he could do was go on with Briggs, pushing forward with the hope that Lawrence or Hainin might have the key to the mystery of who had hired them, a key which Briggs patently did not possess.

The trail moved steadily upward along the flank of the mountain now. Bright blue flowers grew in the broken earth on their left where it fell away in tumbling rocks, wooded slides, and open patches where weeds and buttercups mingled in riotous yellows, greens, and oranges. The pines were thinner up here, and they sighed constantly in the ever-present mountain wind. The trail was covered in a blanket of pine needles dropped through the years, a springy, muffling mat on which the horses' hoofs made hardly any noise. When they crossed a rocky patch, the clatter of the animals feet sounded startlingly loud and echoed slightly against the face of the mountain. As they climbed on upward, the trail leveled out on a plateau gouged into the flank of the slope, rising sharply to one side of them and falling away to the other. Far below, they could follow the boulder-strewn course of a dried-up mountain stream, choked with summer weeds and shrubs. Once in a while they caught sight of deer flickering off on silent feet into deeper forest cover. Squirrels chattered in the trees, whose tops were almost level with their feet. The track often bent around on itself, serpentine in its course up the steepening face of the mountain. Now the trees were thinning behind them, and ahead they could see the end of the tree-line, where jumbled rock and black boulders had been shifted by some primeval glacial upthrust and small patches of unhealthy-looking grassy moss clung to the downhill sides. The trail constantly twisted back on itself as they climbed. Finally they were on the divide and could see El Rito down below them in the valley.

'You figure he'll be there?' Briggs asked. 'What you think, Angel?'

'Damned if I know,' Angel told him. 'He's your sidekick. You tell me. You said he's got a woman up here?'

'Yeah, Mex girl he met down in Lincoln county. Her folks moved up here durin' the troubles. Jamesie often useta ride all the way up here to see her. He was talkin' about marryin' her, one time.'

'She got her own place, or what?'

'I don't know, an' that's Gospel,' Briggs replied. 'I never seen her. All I know is Jamesie allus useta say, any time you want me an' don't know where I'm at, you find Abrana Gutiérrez — an' like as not you'll find me too.'

'Let's hope you're right,' Angel said, concentrating on the trail as it sloped down into the shadowed trees and turned around on itself in a tight S-curve followed farther down by another.

'What you figure to do with the money, Angel?' Briggs asked, as they negotiated the second part of the first bend. He leaned back in the saddle, his head turned toward Angel, who was riding behind him.

'Spend it,' Angel said shortly. He had no time at all for people who dreamed what they would do with money they were never going to have.

'Yeah,' Briggs said, drawing the word out into breathy anticipation. 'Me, I'm gonna head for California, rent me a fancy house overlookin' San Francisco Bay. Stock the cellar full o' French brandy, imported cigars. Have me a time with the ladies. Live the way a man's supposed to live.'

Angel said nothing. He never ceased to be surprised at how modest the ambitions of most criminals were. Boiled down to essentials, they usually amounted to plenty of food, plenty of booze, and plenty of women — although not necessarily in that order. He couldn't concentrate properly on

Briggs's prattling, anyway. His mind was busy with the possible options that lay ahead. Briggs had swallowed Angel's story whole, but that didn't mean Lawrence and Hainin would. He felt an impending sense of disaster, which he could not rationalize, which he felt might have been prompted by the sight of the old plaza in Las Vegas, where not too many years before, he had killed Milt Sharp and Howie Kamins and sat in the room at the hotel afterward trembling like a leaf because he had become a murderer. He had rationalized all that long since: Kamins and Sharp had been frontier vermin of the most pernicious type, and if he hadn't killed them, someone else undoubtedly would have. But the sight of the place and the memory of that night had somehow depressed him. He wondered if Angus Wells, in all his years with the department, had ever felt that way. He acted like a man who had never had a moment's doubt about his right to dispense justice.

'. . . got some mighty handsome women in San Francisco,' Briggs was saying, smiling to himself at the thought of all those lovely pleasures waiting for him in the city by the bay. It was a nice thought to die on, and die he did — the booming thunder of the shot from somewhere up above the first bend of the second S-curve startled Angel's horse, which shied back as Dick Briggs fell out of his saddle as if someone had hit him alongside the head with a huge, invisible club. His horse staggered on the lip of the trail, its feet skittering dirt and stones downward as it fought not to go over after the man who had been shot off its back. Briggs's body fell straight down for about forty feet and then it bounced sickeningly, the broken thud carrying clearly up toward Angel. He was already out of his saddle and flat against the frowning wall on the mountain side of the trail, lifted Winchester in his hands, ears tensely tuned for the sound of movement.

He cursed himself for not having

been on his guard, for now he was not sure from which direction the shot had come. Was the ambusher above and ahead of him? Or above and behind?

He moved out fast from the rock overhang, pumping the lever of the Winchester as he ran down the trail and around the second bend and skidded into a turning fall, the rifle barrel coming up ready to fire at anything behind him.

Nothing. He eased himself upright, skirting the corner of the boulder which formed the shoulder of the bend he had just come around. As he delicately edged forward, his rifle ready for rapid fire, his eyes scanned the faceless jumble of rock and cliff above and around him.

Nothing.

He tried to put himself into the shoes of the ambusher. What would he do? Sit tight. No way his prey could see him until he moved or fired. Yet he could probably see Angel clean and clear the whole time. He could wait.

If he wanted to kill me, Angel thought. But if he only wanted to kill Briggs? Then he'd fade back into the screening timber, moving softly and without haste until he came to wherever he had tied his horse. And he would be gone without Angel ever knowing where he'd been.

If.

Why just Briggs?

There could only be one reason: to cut the connection between him and Angel. Alone, Angel would not know Lawrence, would not be able to convince either him or Hainin that he had been Briggs's rescuer, helper, and partner. Kind of a rough justice, Angel thought wryly. I never was any of those, anyway. Then the second part of the equation occurred to him, and he knew that Briggs had died for another reason, just as he knew with reasonable certainty what he would discover in El Rito.

Lawrence had not had the money, but he had known where Hainin was. So Briggs and Lawrence had become liabilities. And no doubt Jamesie Lawrence was as dead as Briggs, poor Briggs who would never fondle the flesh of the San Francisco whores he had so coveted, who instead lay broken and dead with half of his head gone, at the bottom of a brush-choked canyon a hundred miles from nowhere.

For some obscure reason, the thought angered him. He stepped out into the open, throwing his head back challenging whoever was out there.

'Come on!' he shouted. 'Let me see your face!'

The echoes bounced back off the mountainside, but nothing happened. Nothing moved. Angel shook his head, angry with himself, surprised at his folly. Dick Briggs had been a two-bit paid bandit, and there was no point in grieving for him.

He caught up with his horse and moved on down into El Rito, not looking once into the shadowed gully where Briggs would lie until coyotes and the buzzards arrived.

10

El Rito wasn't much more than a wide place in the trail.

A huddle of unlovely adobes, maybe a dozen in all, scattered the crossroads. The people were all Mexicans, and women with opaque eyes holding impassive babies watched as he rode past the street, then came down into the trail behind him, joining the small children who gathered around his horse and looked up at him with shamelessly hostile curiosity. Not many Anglos came up here, Angel figured, and those who did were not welcome.

Especially now, he amended his thoughts. Especially now.

He did not need to ask for the house of Abrana Gutiérrez, because it was plain that it was the two-room adobe at the end of the street, where a small crowd was gathered. Immobile and offering no help, the men, women, and children all watched the sobbing woman in the doorway, cradling in her arms the bloody head of a man.

Jamesie Lawrence.

Angel swung down from the saddle and pushed his way through the knot of people. They made way for him sullenly, unwillingly, resentful of his intrusion. The woman looked up at him with streaming eyes. Her face was swollen, knotted with grief, and he detested himself for what he had to do.

'Abrana?' he asked. 'Abrana Gutiérrez?'

'*Sí*,' she nodded, her voice broken and old. '*Sí*.'

'*Soy Ricardo Briggs, un amigo de Jaime*,' he told her, biting on the lie that he was either a friend of the dead man or Dick Briggs in person.

'Yes,' she said in Spanish. 'Much good it will do him.'

'Will you tell me what happened?'

'I will tell you later,' she said. 'Tomorrow. Go away now. Come back tomorrow.'

'Yes,' an old woman standing to one side said. 'Go away. Come back tomorrow. Can't you leave us alone, you murderers?'

There was a mutter of angry agreement from the men.

'Abrana,' Angel said gently, stooping beside the weeping woman. 'Let me help you. He's dead. There's nothing more you can do for him.'

She lifted her face to him again and saw something in his eyes, something that made her nod wordlessly and release the dead man's cradled head. Jamesie Lawrence's sightless eyes stared up at the unheeding sky. He had been shot at point-blank range through the heart, Angel noted almost dispassionately; there were powder burns on the woolen shirt, and the bullet hole was sharp and black-edged. Then a coup de grace in the back of the head. The Easterner was a professional, who took no chances, Angel thought. No chances at all.

He motioned to one of the Mexicans,

taking hold of Lawrence's body beneath the arms. The man reluctantly took Lawrence's feet, and they carried him into the bedroom and put him on the bed. Angel straightened up and thanked the Mexican, who crossed himself and left the room without speaking. The place was a shambles. Cupboards had been torn open, shelves had been ripped off the walls, and the mattress itself was slashed and cut in several places. Each piece of furniture looked as if it had been savagely, methodically attacked, broken, and discarded. He went into the other room, where if anything the wreckage was worse. Broken china strewed the floor, crunching beneath his feet as he entered. Abrana Gutiérrez sat in a wooden chair, weeping softly, her face cradled in her hands.

'Tell me what happened,' he asked her. 'Maybe I can help.'

'You can bring him back to life, perhaps?' she asked bitterly. 'You can give me back my man?'

'Tell me,' he said again. 'Tell me who did this.'

'I do not know,' she confessed. 'Jaime . . . we were in the fields. There was much work to do. Corn to mill. We came back to the house, and Jaime went in. The man must have been waiting inside. I heard them talking. Then they started to argue, and I heard Jaime shouting the words 'cheat' and 'liar.' Then the other man said, 'Where is he?' and Jaime told him to go to hell. They started to fight and I ran in. The man reached into his pocket, here — ' She indicated her left hip, 'and there was a gun. He shot. He shot . . . ' Her voice broke and she started sobbing again.

Angel let her cry. If she'd seen Jamesie Lawrence shot that close, it would be many years before she forgot it, and it was better that she weep and weep and weep than that she started to think about what it might have felt like for him, smashed backward against the

132

adobe wall with his heart literally blown apart.

'Tell me about the man,' he said, after a while.

'A big man,' she said, wiping her eyes. 'Almost as big as you. Perhaps the same. I could not see his face very well. Cruel, a sharp face. He wore black clothes. A cape, like a matador.'

'You see what color his eyes were, or his hair? Anything like that?'

'No, señor. After he — when I saw Jaime fall, I ran at this man with my hands to kill him. He hit me hard with something, here — ' She turned her head, and he saw the dark bruise under the hairline above her right ear. 'When I woke up, he was gone. And the house was like this.'

'Do you know why he came here, Abrana?'

'Sí,' she nodded dully. 'The money. It was the money, no?'

Angel nodded. 'It was the money.'

'I told them to send it back. It was too much. That much money is alive, it is evil, I said. It can destroy you. Pedro was here. He laughed.'

'You mean Pete Hainin?'

'Sí,' she answered.

'You know where he is now?'

Her eyes went opaque.

'You do know,' Angel said. 'Tell me, then, if you will not say where he is — did Jamesie know?' She nodded.

'Did he have it written down someplace?'

Her eyes flickered involuntarily toward the mantel and widened as she realized something, She hesitated for a moment, then rose, moving swiftly across the room. She rummaged in the debris on the floor and finally found, a splintered cigar box. Its lid hung loose. It was empty.

'He has it,' she said, defeat in her voice.

Then it all came out. Lawrence and Hainin had obviously decided to play it safe once they knew for sure that Dick Briggs wouldn't be joining them. They had put the money in a locked suitcase and checked it aboard a train out of

Santa Fe. The suitcase would be held at the depot in Trinidad for collection. Then they had ceremonially divided the claim check into two halves. Hainin had taken one half, Jamesie Lawrence the other. They had cut across the printed number on the check so that one half was useless without its mate. Then Hainin had gone, leaving his whereabouts scribbled on the back of Lawrence's half of the claim check.

'A hotel,' Abrana Gutiérrez said. 'In Santa Fe. The name . . . the name . . . ?'

Angel told her the names of three he knew, but it was none of those.

'It was an unusual name,' she said. 'It sounded like what Anglos say, good day, how are you?'

'It doesn't matter,' he told her. 'Abrana, I have to try to get to Pete Hainin before the man who was here does, or he will kill him. You understand this?'

'Sí,' she said, her voice that of a woman who has been told many lies. No longer young, no longer pretty,

135

Abrana Gutierrez had lost her whole world when Jamesie Lawrence had put up a fight for his one hope to make it into the big money. The easterner wasn't the kind you could back off with hard talk. And he had a damned fine head start to Santa Fe that Angel would be very lucky to reduce. He glanced out of the little window. The sky was a dirty gray above the mountains, and there was a fresh wind springing up.

'Abrana, I must go,' he said. 'But I would wish to bury Jamesie properly. And to care for you as well as I may. This is the gift of a friend. You will honor me by accepting it.'

He held out the bundle of notes which he'd picked up back at the La Fonda, and she looked at them and then into his eyes and then back at the money.

'I . . .'

'Take it,' he said, thrusting it into her hand. He went out of the house and beneath the hating glances of the people standing outside, crossed the street to his horse. Then Abrana Gutiérrez came to the door. 'Briggs!' she shouted.

For a moment he failed to react, and then he turned.

'Helloes,' she said. 'That was it — helloes.'

He lifted a hand; Herlow's was a ratbag hotel on San Francisco Street — the kind of place you stayed in when your money was really tight. It figured Hainin would be somewhere like that. He only hoped he had half a chance of getting there before the Easterner did.

He rode out of El Rito in a silence you could touch.

11

Burro Alley, they called it, a thorough-fare of hock-deep dust and ramshackle one-story adobes, which were dilapidated and run-down. There were mules tethered everywhere: most of the freighting outfits had some kind of an office on Burro Alley, hence its nickname. As his horse picked its way through the litter, discarded tin cans, rain-sodden copies of the *New Mexican*, and the broken wooden crates tossed out of the nearest window and left to rot where they fell, the sun broke through the heavy cloud on the horizon and Angel felt the warmth of a copper sun. It was still cool — the Royal City of the Holy Faith of St Francis of Assisi was built on a plateau of the Sangre de Cristos, a good seven thousand feet above sea level. But now the gray storm clouds, which had threatened to burst since leaving El Rito, were sliding off to the east, leaving the sky a deep cerulean blue. The streets gave off the dank odor of evaporating rainwater, a visible moisture rising from the pitted, ordured dust. A slouching man came out of the door of a *cantina*, and the sour smell of stale liquor spread in the humid air. La Paloma, the place was called. Then another cantina, Cielo Azul, and another, La Golondrina. There were shuttered windows on many of the huddled adobes, but the doors were open. Inside he could see the women yawning. Burro Alley was a place of the night, not fit to be seen by day.

He turned south between two of the crack-faced adobes and came out onto San Francisco Street. He saw the sign almost immediately: 'P.F. HERLOW — ROOMS DAILY OR WEEKLY RATES.' He slid off his horse outside and gratefully stretched his cramped legs. It had been a long ride.

It was dark and cool inside the rambling adobe. There was a rough deal counter on one side of the doorway built across what had perhaps been an alcove. A corridor lay straight ahead, curtained off. Angel could see the doors of rooms on each side of it.

The man at the counter watched him with unabashed curiosity. He was a thick-faced, square-jawed man with the shrewd eyes of a pimp. He spoke with a German accent, rasping a reflective thumb across a three day stubble when he heard the name of the person Angel was asking for.

'Hainin, Hainin,' he said, aloud. 'Dot's his name?'

'Come on,' Angel said. 'I don't have all day.'

'Hainin,' the man said again, reflectively.

Angel didn't have time to waste, and he lost his temper. He grabbed the front of the man's shirt and hauled him half over the counter. 'What room is he in, damn you?'

Bug-eyed and astonished, the clerk wriggled and struggled in vain against

Angel's grip. 'Zeven,' he gasped. 'Zeven.'

Angel let him go, and the man's boots thumped back on the packed, earthern floor.

He was slapping the tatty curtain aside and going into the hallway as the man called, 'Ze ozzer man said don't — '

Angel wheeled around and came back to the desk. 'Other man?' he rasped. 'What other man?'

'Ze ozzer American,' faltered the man behind the.eaunter. 'He came earlier. Iss still zere, I sink.'

Angel slid the gun from his holster, and the man's eyes bugged again. He looked as if he expected the gun in Angel's hand to attack him on its own.

'What's your name?' Angel asked.

'Herlow,' the man told him. 'Peter Herlow. This my place.'

'All right, Herlow,' Angel said tersely. 'Here's what you do. Run as if your life depended on it. Get the sheriff or the marshal. Tell them there's been a murder here.'

'Murder?' Herlow managed. 'Here?'

'Go on,' Angel said. 'Get going!'

Herlow looked at Angel's face, and what he saw seemed to convince him that the most sensible place he could be was outside his own hotel and on his way to the sheriff. This cold-eyed American who spoke of murder didn't give the impression of being a man who'd joke about such things. He lifted the hinged counter uneasily and slid beneath it, his eyes never leaving Angel's revolver. Then he nodded nervously once, twice and bolted for the doorway.

Angel slid cat-footed into the hallway, moving along the rush matting on light feet until he came to the door with a rough figure seven painted on it. Edging up close to the wall, he cocked his ears for any sound coming from the room. Nothing but silence and the far-off sound of a woman laughing in another house down the street.

He kicked the door open and went in on one knee, the Colt cocked and only his thumb holding the hammer back.

The place was empty, featureless. A typical adobe cell: a sagging bed with a mud-colored blanket; a commode beside it with a sooty-chimneyed oil lamp standing on top; a cupboard in the corner of the room built into the wall, its green door slightly ajar. Nothing else.

He was across the room in two strides. He pulled the cupboard door open. Hainin was jammed inside, his head between his knees, his arms at his sides, in the position an exhausted runner sometimes takes when he falls out of a gruelling race. Hainin had fallen out of the most gruelling race of all.

Grunting with exertion, Angel man-handled the body out of the cupboard and managed to sling the dead robber face downward on the protesting bed. There was blood on Angel's hands, and he wiped them clean on the dead man's shirt, swiftly checking Hainin's pockets, knowing he would find nothing.

He turned the man over. Hainin's

face still bore an expression of faint surprise, as though he had not been quite prepared for death. He had been killed professionally, Angel noted; there was only the one thick-lipped knife wound just to the right of and below the sternum. A long-bladed knife would have slid into Hainin's heart as smoothly as if oiled, its wicked inner rigidity razoring the astonished heart to instant silence. Hainin hadn't even bled a lot, although there was a thick coagulating puddle on the floor of the cupboard.

Angel turned quickly and checked the drawer of the commode — an empty Durham sack, some matches, an oilskin wallet containing money, about thirty dollars, and a photograph of a long-haired woman in a bell-shaped dress, standing with one hand resting on the arm of a sofa. The legend below the photograph read 'Gainborough Studios, El Paso.' Angel looked under the bed and found an army duffle bag with Hainin's clothes clumsily stuffed into it — Hainin's killer had obviously checked that. Something gleamed. He stretched beneath the bed, and his fingers touched metal. It was a straight-bladed dirk, what they called a Mexican knife. The blade was seven inches long and as sharp as a razor. Around the hilt were the sticky traces of Hainin's blood. Angel stood with it in his hand, knowing it would tell him nothing — you could buy a knife like this in any hardware store in the southwest for a couple of dollars. With a gesture of disgust he hefted the knife and threw it down, driving its point deep into the top of the commode. The knife spanged shivering into the wood. It was still quivering when the deep voice at the door told Angel to stand very, very still.

He stood still while his gun was lifted from his holster. Hands patted his body: their owner knew where a man might keep a hideaway gun or a knife, and he wasn't a bit concerned about embarrassing his captive. But Angel had no knife or gun hidden on him, and after a moment he was told to turn around.

'Name?'

His questioner was a stocky, almost portly man of about five feet seven, dressed in ordinary blue work pants and a white cotton shirt. His open vest was held together by a looping metal watchchain, which started at a horizontal silver bar slipped through the buttonhole on the left side and ended in a bulging pocket on the right. The waistcoat had old-fashioned lapels, and on one of these was pinned a five-pointed star with the word Sheriff engraved on it in script.

'Angel, Frank Angel,' Angel told him. 'Sheriff, I'm glad you're here — this man's been murdered.'

He saw Herlow peering at him from behind the sheriff, pimp's eyes taking in the whole scene with vicious satisfaction.

'Well,' the sheriff said in his unexpectedly deep voice. 'As to that, I'm sorta glad I'm here too, Mister Angel. Sure as Satan didn't figure he'd died from old age, there.'

'He was dead when I got in here,' Angel said. 'You can see for yourself. Whoever killed him stuck him in that cupboard there. I just dragged him out before you came.'

'Sure,' the Sheriff said. 'You want to try the other leg, now?'

Angel looked at him for a long moment and then at Herlow. His face set.

'What did he tell you?' he said.

'Who, Herlow? Said some feller come into his hotel, asked for a guest who'd told 'im nobody knew he was here an' that was the way he wanted to keep it, an' then said he should go get the sheriff 'cause they was goin' to be a murder done.'

Angel nodded, acknowledging his own stupidity. The Easterner was out-thinking him all along the line.

'And of course, you came in here to find me with blood on my hands, the

147

dead man with his pockets turned out, and the murder weapon right there for you to use as exhibit number one for the territory.'

'Boy, you're half-smart for someone done somethin' this dumb,' the sheriff said.

'Herlow didn't mention the other man who was in here just before me?'

The sheriff raised his eyebrows. Without taking his eyes off Angel, he said, 'Herlow?'

'Sheriff?'

'Was some other guy in here before our visitin' Angel, here?'

'No, sir.'

'Let me talk to him . . . ' Angel said, starting to move forward. Herlow shrank back, fear washing his face white, but Angel stopped in mid-stride, the sheriff's gun jammed into his belly.

'Don't you be an old silly-billy, now,' the sheriff said gently.

'All right,' Angel said. 'All right.'

He took a step back, hands held at mid-bicep level.

'I'm going to get something in a pocket in my belt, Sheriff,' he said. 'OK?'

'What is it?'

'It's a badge,' Angel said. 'just a badge.'

'Get it,' the sheriff said, curiosity on his face now. 'But get it slow.'

Angel unnotched his belt, and from the slit pocket on the right hand side above his hip, he produced a circular silver badge. He tossed it on the bed where the sheriff could see it. The watery sun coming in through the deep-walled window caught highlights on the embossed lettering, *Department of Justice, United States of America*.

The sheriff looked at it and then at Angel.

'You might've stole that,' he said, reasonably.

Angel was already unfolding a parchment from the thin oilskin in which it had been wrapped. He handed it to the sheriff, who took it with his left hand.

'That paper says I'm a special

investigator for the Department of Justice, acting on direct instructions from the attorney general of the United States. One part of it somewhere says that all federal and territorial officers are requested to give me their fullest cooperation and assistance in all matters.'

'You could've stole this, too,' the sheriff said.

'I could be Billy the Kid as well,' Angel said. 'But I'm not. Look at that bastard's face an' tell me he told you the truth!'

The sheriff looked at Angel dubiously. He wasn't going to fall for any of those tricks. He was good at what he did, and he was able to keep on being so by never falling for the old dodges. He took a step back until his shoulders touched the wall. Now he could see both Angel and Herlow.

'Well, Herlow,' he snapped. 'What about it?'

'Listen,' Herlow faltered. 'I didn't know. It — he — '

'All right,' Angel rasped. 'Let's hear all of it, Herlow!'

Cornered, Herlow gabbled it all out, stuttering in his anxiety to tell it all as fast as he could, to get out from under the basilisk glare of the sheriff, whose name, Angel now learned for the first time, was Hogben.

Herlow told them that the first man, the big American who had come into the hotel perhaps an hour before Frank Angel, had asked for Hainin. Hainin had paid Herlow twenty dollars to say to anyone who came asking for him that he was not there and then to tip him off so he could check out whoever it was before revealing himself. But the big American had said, 'Tell me the room number, nothing more,' and when Herlow had professed ignorance, he had started counting ten dollar gold pieces out onto the counter, stopping each time he added five to the growing pile to ask once again for the room number, nothing else. When the pile was three hundred dollars, he stopped and straightened. Herlow, fearing that this fortune in gold was about to be swept from beneath his nose, had blurted out Hainin's room number. The American had nodded.

'Something else,' he had said quietly. 'In a short while, perhaps two or three hours, no more, another American will come here asking for Hainin.' He had described Angel perfectly, then continued, 'You will tell him that I am still in the room with Hainin. Nothing else. You understand?' Herlow had said he understood, and the American had then told him that Angel would probably question him about who the first man had been and what he looked like or send for the sheriff or the US Marshal or both. If he claimed to be a government investigator, he was lying. He was, in fact, an escaped convict named Briggs, who had broken out of Folsom Penitentiary a few days back and was wanted for attempted murder. Herlow would be able to claim the reward, and there would be no risk involved, no risk at all.

'Unless,' the big man had told him, 'you fail to do exactly as I say. Should that happen, Herlow, I would of course feel it necessary to come back to Santa Fe and kill you.'

He had said this so coldly, his words such a calm and unemotional statement of deadly intent, that Herlow had devoutly believed him and signaled his agreement. Then the man had gone down the corridor and into Hainin's room. There had been no noise, no sound of a struggle, nothing. He had not, truly, seen the man leave the hotel. But of course, he had gone across the street for a couple of drinks to celebrate his windfall.

'Brother,' the sheriff said when Herlow had finished talking. 'If that don't muddy the water, I don't know what does!'

Angel stifled his disappointment and chagrin. Once again the Easterner had outthought him, setting Herlow up with a story which he had told so patently

153

and blatantly that Herlow had swallowed it hook, line and sinker. It was just right, contrived so artfully that no matter what evidence he produced to the contrary, the sheriff was going to have to check with Folsom before he could release Angel.

And that would take time, and time was all that Angel's quarry needed.

He had the two halves of the claim check now. All he had to do was get to Trinidad and collect the suitcase.

'Hogben, what trains are there to Trinidad?' he asked unexpectedly.

'One a day, but you ain't takin' it,' Hogben said.

'What time?' Angel asked impatiently. 'What time does it pull out?'

Sheriff Hogben delved into the bulging waistcoat pocket with his left hand — all this time he had kept his drawn six-gun more or less generally pointing in Angel's direction — and pressed the lid of his watch.

'Leaves at midday,' he said, as if reading it from the face of the watch.

'About four hours ago.'

'That's right,' Hogben confirmed. 'She gets up there, oh, 'bout nine or nine-thirty, dependin' on how things go.'

He looked levelly at Angel, then glared at Herlow again.

'Damn if I know what to make of all this,' he muttered. 'You say you're some kind of investigator for the Department of Justice. This other feller said you was an escaped felon.'

'This other fellow killed Hainin,' Angel pointed out. 'Didn't he?'

'As to that,' Hogben said, cocking his head to one side wryly, 'that's how it looks on the face of it. But you ain't said why.'

Angel picked up his badge, folded the Justice Department commission, and stowed them in his pocket.

'Is John Sherman in town?' he asked.

The sheriff looked startled. John T. Sherman was the United States Marshal for the territory.

'*You* know him?'

'No,' Angel said. 'But we've got mutual friends. And he's got priority call on the telegraph if he needs it. Maybe we can clear this up that way.'

Hogben pursed his lips. 'Well,' he said.

'Sheriff,' Angel said levelly. 'You could be right. I might be Briggs, I might be wanted by Folsom. In which case, you've got me anyway. But if you're wrong — and you are — you're going to get the biggest black mark in your copybook anyone's ever seen. You'll be lucky if they let you run for dog-catcher. Now don't you figure it's worth the trouble to check?'

'Well,' Hogben hesitated.

'Sheriff,' Angel said, and there was no pleading in his voice any more, no anxiety, nothing but a flat certainty. 'I don't want to have to kill you to get out of here now, but if I have to, I will.'

Hogben looked at Angel's eyes, then down at the gun in his own hand, and then back at Angel with a new expression. He damned well thinks he could do it, he thought to himself. He thinks he could come at a man with a gun in his hand three feet away and kill him. And in the same moment he realized that this was no ordinary fugitive cane-breaker.

'All right,' he said, thrusting his six-gun into its holster. 'Herlow, lock this place up. Nobody in or out, understand? I'll likely want to talk to you again!' The way he said it made Herlow cringe, but the hotel keeper nodded, rubbing his hands together anxiously.

'Angel,' Sheriff Hogben said. 'Let's go!'

12

The big man knew he was clear now.

He sat in the plushly upholstered Pullman car of the Atchison Topeka & Sante Fe train laboring up the long, rising incline across the flank of the Turkey Mountains, satisfied that he had covered everything, delayed pursuit sufficiently, and given himself more than enough time to do what needed to be done. Each time the train swayed around a curve, he could see the snowy peaks of the Sangre de Cristo Mountains, some of their peaks fourteen thousand feet high, the fresh snow pink in the light of the sun sliding through the western sky. Up ahead lay the Raton Pass, and twenty-five miles beyond that, Trinidad, Colorado.

There was no one left now who could connect him with the money; no one, that was, except Frank Angel. He knew the man well enough to know that the delaying tactics he had spread in Angel's path would slow his pursuit but not stop it. Never stop it. He might get clear of Trinidad with the money, but Angel would never stop looking for him and never forget. So Angel must die. He did not want to kill Angel. Yet he could see no alternative, and so he had arranged that, too. Angel knew where he was heading — Trinidad. Therefore, he would come to Trinidad. Probably on the next day's train — he would get help in Santa Fe; they would confirm who he was very quickly. Perhaps even a special train? It was no matter. The three men would wait at the railway station, and when Angel came, they would kill him. It would not be a matter of stupid Anglo-Saxon manners, of 'even breaks' and facing the man you were about to kill. The three killers were *ladrones*, who murdered for gain, from cover, by stealth, at night, without warning, in ambush — murdered only when it was safe for themselves, when no risk was obtained, when the victim had no warning.

It was a pity; but if he was ever to know peace, Angel must die.

He thought ahead, anticipating his route. From Trinidad through Denver to Cheyenne, Wyoming. From there by stagecoach to Salt Lake City, and from the Mormon capital by easy stretches, sometimes on horseback, sometimes by buggy, others by public transport, across the country to Portland, Oregon. Then to Seattle and by ferry from there to Vancouver. He had been there once when he was a very young man and had fallen in love with the long, silent fjords, the majestic pine-clad mountains on their sides. Across the bay from Vancouver was the very British settlement of Victoria, its kaleidoscope of colored, wooden houses sloping gently down to the water's edge, the snowy grandeur of the mountains astonishing and ghost-like as they soared above the flat gray clouds across the Gulf of Georgia.

There he would buy a house, hire a housekeeper — maybe after a decent interval marry her, if she were pleasant enough — and live the life of a country squire amidst the gossiping, inbred British settlers. A man could live very well on the income from $250,000, very well indeed. Well enough to leave the capital untouched for his sons. He was still young enough, man enough, to spawn a litter of them if he felt the urge. He allowed himself a thin smile at his own daydreams. All in good time, he told himself, all in good time.

And only when Angel is dead.

* * *

The message came chattering back over the wires, the key stuttering as the telegrapher scribbled furiously to write it down. They read it over his shoulder:

SHERMAN MARSHAL SANTA FE STOP GIVE INSTANT PRIORITY ASSISTING FRANK ANGEL STOP IDENTIFY HIM

BY CODED SIGNATURE RECEIVED
FROM HIM THROUGH YOU CONFI-
DENTIAL THIS DEPARTMENT STOP
BUT IF STILL IN DOUBT ASK HIM
NAME HIS LANDLADY STOP WAIT-
ING.

It was signed by the attorney general.

'Mrs Rissick,' Angel told them. 'Mrs
Maureen Rissick.'

The telegrapher tapped out the reply
and then switched off. They waited,
imagining the looping wires that
hummed in the moaning winds across
the thousands of miles to the ugly old
building on Pennsylvania Avenue. They
jumped, startled, when the key began
chattering again, as if it were angry. The
telegrapher began to scribble furiously.

ANSWER CORRECT THAT'S ANGEL
STOP ASK HIM WHERE THE HELL
HE THINKS HE HAS BEEN QUES-
TION MARK NO REPORT SINCE
DEPARTURE STOP DOES HE THINK
WE'RE TELEPATHIC QUESTION

MARK RENDER ALL NECESSARY ASSISTANCE ON MY PERSONAL AUTHORITY STOP BY THIS I MEAN YOU WILL DO WHATEVER ANGEL SAYS YOU ARE TO DO STOP TRUST MESSAGE CLEAR STOP AWAIT REPORT FROM ANGEL.

Frank Angel grinned. He could visualize the attorney general in his office, puffing furiously on one of his awful cigars as he stamped up and down dictating his message to his personal private secretary, Amabel Rowe. He let his thoughts linger on the memory of her honey-blonde hair spilling back in the sunlight and her light laughter. But only for a moment.

Then he turned to Sherman.

'Happy?' he asked.

'Hell, Angel,' Sheriff Hogben said. 'We had to check. You understand, it wasn't anything personal.'

'Forget it,' Angel said brusquely. He didn't have time for hurt feelings, his own or anyone else's. All he was conscious of now was the time that had been wasted, the miles lost, the distance between him and his quarry.

'I want a telegraph sent to Trinidad,' he said. 'Whoever you know: deputy US Marshal, local sheriff . . . ?'

'Sheriff up there's a friend of mine,' Hogben put in, eager now to make amends. 'Cecil Smith. Smithy, everyone calls him.'

'Good, fine,' Angel said. 'I want the baggage office at the railway depot covered by at least three men. They're to watch for anyone like our man coming in to claim a suitcase. I'll write down a description for you.'

'You want him taken, or what?' Sherman asked.

'Only if he tries to leave Trinidad,' Angel said. 'I figure he probably will, but I don't know which way, so they'd better keep a damned close eye on him.'

'I'll tell 'em,' Sherman said grimly. 'Don't you worry none.'

'Something else,' Angel continued. 'I want the top local man from the A. T. &

S. F. railway, and I want him fast!'

'Bob Gray,' Sheriff Hogben said. 'I'll go get him.'

He started out but was stopped by a word from Angel.

'Tell him I want a special train,' Angel said. 'Fastest engine he's got, the best engineer. We're going to break the record for getting from here to Trinidad, and I don't want anything fouling me up. Tell him I'll want every inch of the track from here to there clean. Understand me? *Clean*! I don't even want to see a dead chicken on it. Tell him I want the track cleared so we can run up there the whole way, no stops, nothing.'

'You'll need to stop for water,' Sherman pointed out. 'Fuel, maybe.'

'Tell him to lay it on,' Angel said. 'He'll know where, how much. But fast. Faster than he's ever done it before.'

'It'll take a bit of doing,' Hogben said, dubiously.

'Then you'd best not waste any more time,' Angel told him. The sheriff blinked and nodded, turning to almost run out of the marshal's office into the darkening plaza outside. Angel watched him weaving between the idling walkers and disappear around the obelisk commemorating the soldiers who had fallen in the battle of Valverde.

'You want to let me have that description now, Angel?' Sherman called from the telegrapher's room. 'We're ready to send.'

Angel nodded and went in, hitching his hip on the corner of the telegrapher's desk.

'Six feet even,' he said. 'Dark blond hair, blue eyes. Wears a mustache, also dark blond, but he may have shaved that off. Last seen wearing dark suit, black cape. Like a matador's,' he said, remembering what Abrana Gutiérrez had said. 'Which could mean it's got a red silk lining. He may also be disguising the fact that he has a limp, favoring the right leg. Uses his left hand more than the right — any gun will be on that side. And tell them to be very,

very careful if they go after him. He's a crack shot, an expert knife fighter. And he can kill men with his bare hands.'

'By God, Angel,' Sherman said. 'You sound as if you know him.'

'I'm beginning to think I do,' Angel replied.

He went back into the outer office and pulled a pad of telegraph blanks toward him. Picking up a pencil, he wrote the words 'Personal Attention of the Attorney General Only.' Then he put what he knew and what he suspected into words.

13

It was Vargas who spotted the *Norteamericano* first. He hissed a warning to Chávez and Montoya and jerked his chin at the three men coming down Guadalupe Street toward the railroad depot.

Two of them they knew very well already: John Sherman and the sheriff, Mike Hogben. The third fit exactly the description of the man they planned to kill.

The depot was an adobe building with a long canopied ramada similar to the one outside the Palace of the Governors — the same *viga* poles, the same three-foot thick adobe pillars, the same rounded corners, even the same apathetic Indians from San Ildefonso or Santo Domingo, their wrists jangling with bracelets, their arms burdened with gaily striped blankets. The three lawmen came on with long, purposeful strides as an elderly looking, white-haired man came bustling out of the office to the right of the loading platform and hurried toward them.

'Here comes Gray now,' Hogben said.

Robert Gray, district supervisor for the Atchison Topeka & Santa Fe Railroad, bustled toward them, mopping his brow even though it was scarcely a few hours past dawn.

'Mister Angel?' he said. 'I'm Robert Gray, and I want to tell you that I've never been put to so much trouble in all my years with the Santa Fe. Why, do you know my Head Office . . . ?'

Angel let the man babble on, not really listening to him, intent on seeing for himself whether the engine was ready to go. Through the dark-shadowed arches he could see a locomotive at the siding. An engineer in a blue-striped coat was leaning out of the side with the kind of expression men have on their faces when they've been told to hurry and then have to hang around waiting for the people who told them to hurry.

'You've cleared the right-of-way?' Angel asked, cutting across Gray's self-justifying chatter. 'All the way up the line?'

'Yes, yes, you've no idea how difficult it was,' Gray said. 'I've been up most of the night, what with one thing and another . . .'

Jabber, jabber, jabber, Angel thought; what does he think we've been doing all night, drinking tequila and chasing whores? His eyes were gritty from the hours spent waiting by the telegraph. Each time it erupted into spiteful chatter, it demanded more justification, detail, and evidence which he had no way of providing.

The evidence was in Trinidad, Colorado. The only way he could prove his case was to go there and get it. He said it again and again by means of the telegraph, and finally, almost as if wearying of the argument, the machine had clattered the attorney general's permission. Given, if he knew the old man, with the utmost reluctance. But given. He knew that the feverish activity he had begun in Washington would continue, the checking and double-checking would go on until something was found. But in the meantime he was alone again, the way he preferred it. He shook hands with Sherman and Hogben, thanking them for all they had done.

'This way, Mister Angel,' Gray said, going ahead into the depot. 'The engine's waiting.'

He gestured toward the panting locomotive on the far side of the yard and turned as if to lead him on.

'That'll be fine, Mister Gray,' Angel said, 'just fine. No need for you to get your shoes all muddy out there.'

Gray looked at his spotless shoes and then at Angel's scuffed and dirty mule-ears. He frowned. It was true, the ground around and between the right-of-ways was filthy with oil spill,

171

charcoal, coal ash, and soot. Even though Santa Fe was a spur line — the main track ran through Lamy, ten miles to the south, and up through the Glorieta Pass via Cañoncito — they got enough traffic up here to filth the place up, no matter how much time and wasted breath he spent telling the engineers and their crews not to let people use the facilities when the train was in the depot, no matter how often he raked them over the coals for throwing out their oil-stained rags and their cigar butts.

'Very well, Mister Angel,' he said.

Angel nodded and stepped down off the depot platform, quartering across the rails toward the engine. The depot building was a squat oblong facing east. Behind it was a long platform with steps leading down to two passenger platforms. The carriage shed hulked black and gloomy on the north-western corner of the area. There were three sets of buffers behind the depot and four on the northern edge of the yard. There the rolling stock awaiting loading or unloading could be switched to keep the passenger bays free. Between these lines and the passenger bays was a water tower, perhaps twenty feet high, which loomed now over four empty flatbed trucks standing on the farthest incoming passenger line. Angel walked the passenger platform alongside these wagons, heading for the open area west of the water tower where the waiting locomotive stood. And every inch of the way, from the time he stepped off the platform with Robert Gray, who was watching his retreating back uncertainly, Angel was in the sights of three rifles. Vargas had the best spot.

He had climbed the water tower and was stretched flat on the platform which ran around it, his body curved a little uncomfortably but with plenty of room for his cradled elbows and the Winchester with which he was going to kill the Anglo. Across on the southern side of the yard was a switchbox, a crude cover for the control levers. It stood about two feet high and behind it, kneeling, Montoya steadied his rifle, waiting for Vargas's signal. Over on the south side of the depot, where the rear platform hugged the southern wall of the building, he knew that Chavez was crouching behind a pile of wooden crates, awaiting the next downhill train.

Angel was out in the open now. No cover — he was about fifty yards from the platform and roughly the same distance from the panting engine. Vargas adjusted his elbow slightly, took a deep breath, and gently squeezed the trigger of the Winchester, leading slightly to compensate for Angel's purposefully swift walk. The other two opened up almost simultaneously, and Angel went down as if he had been hit by a thunderbolt. Vargas was already clambering down the metal rungs of the ladder on the side of the water tower. Montoya and Chavez leaped to their feet, running across the tracks where the fallen Angel lay, aiming past the dead man for the same place for which

Vargas was now scuttling — a wooden stairway at the northern edge of the yards. All they had to do then was jump over a low barbed wire fence that wouldn't have stopped a three-year-old.

Gray's squalling shouts brought Marshal Sherman and Sheriff Hogben thundering through the depot building and to a skidding stop beside the quaking rail-road man.

'They just shot him!' he screeched. 'Look at them running, there, there!'

Sherman and Hogben were already moving, guns drawn. Sherman ran around the far side of the water tower to try to intercept Vargas, who was now crossing the siding and about halfway over. Hogben ran straight to where Angel lay in the middle of the passenger bay. The two Mexicans veered off toward the west when they saw him coming, and Hogben threw a shot at them. They were more than thirty yards away, however, and he didn't expect to hit anything. They were almost in a straight line ahead of him now, leaping across the second pair of rails when Hogben saw Angel rise off the ground. The two Mexicans shied away as if a dinosaur had suddenly spiraled up from nowhere, one of them working the lever of his Winchester furiously, whipping the carbine around to try another shot at this apparently indestructible man.

He never had a chance.

Angel's hand had flickered toward his hip with a speed that defied sight, and the gun was up and spouting fire. The rolling boom of the shots was like a short clap of thunder. Hogben saw the first Mexican catapult backward, his Winchester flying into the air. He fell in a twisting circle in dream-like motion, his face wiped away by the two heavy caliber bullets. The second man was falling even as the first went down, slapped off his feet as though someone seventy feet tall had hit him with a flat plank wielded horizontally.

Hogben ran toward Angel, but the tall man waved him back, gesturing to Sherman's direction. Hogben twisted around, scrambled between the connections of two of the standing flatcars, and came out beside the water tower. He could see Sherman crouched behind the farthest set of buffers on the siding, his six-gun coughing. The third assassin was bayed at the base of the wooden stairs, which Sherman's fleet-footed pursuit had prevented him from climbing in time. Hogben ran quickly toward the buffers, vaulting over them and coming up alongside Sherman, combining his own six-gun fire with the marshal's. The assassin shifted desperately: his position was insecure, the ancient wooden stairs no protection against the smashing impact of the lawmen's bullets. Vargas broke and ran.

Dodging and weaving, panicking as if a trapped bird was caught in his throat, he ran like a rabbit toward the looming carriage shed, to the safety of thick walls and dark corners, to the bolt-hole of open ends and shrouding brush on all sides of it. He ran knowing that his life depended upon getting there, and he bent every single ounce of effort and concentration he possessed.

He wasn't more than twenty yards from the yawning entrance to the sheds when he saw Angel coming across the lines. He knew it was impossible, knew his shot could not have missed, yet here was the dead man running across to intercept him, pistol in hand.

Without breaking stride, he levered the Winchester and threw a shot at Angel, but it was panicked and wide. Angel acknowledged the shot merely by swerving slightly in his run. Vargas levered the Winchester again and flinched when he saw Angel's hand move. The six-gun boomed, and the earth erupted a foot from Vargas' left leg. Squealing with fear, he leaped into a run, dashing like a rabbit across Angel's path. He saw the engineer clambering down from the train, shouting something, but the white fear drove him blindly forward. Ten yards, *Dios, por favor!* Only ten yards! He saw the tall man go down on one knee, leveling the six-gun, both hands clasped solidly around the butt, elbow resting on his right knee, and he knew that he was dead. But no shot came.

With a gesture of disgust, Angel looked at the empty gun in his hand. He was on his feet again, although this time he lurched slightly as he moved. Vargas was no more than twenty feet from him, perhaps the same distance from the carriage shed. Angel paused to touch the side of his boot where the throwing knife was nestled. He shook his head. He was good. But not good enough to hit a running man at that kind of distance. He stood waiting until Sherman and Hogben came panting up, their feet crunching on the oily gravel. Both men were winded, perspiration streaming from their faces.

'In the name of God, Angel!' Sherman said. The entire side of Angel's body was a pulsing mass of blood from the wound Vargas had given him. It should have killed him. The bullet had ploughed into his body just

179

below and behind his right arm, where the long solid muscle was ripped as if by some ugly predator. He had been lucky; the bullet had hit a rib, and instead of turning inward, it had ricocheted outward, ripping a lacerated tear perhaps seven inches long across the front of Frank Angel's chest. Montoya's bullet had torn a hole through the flapping tail of his coat. Chavez had missed, God alone knew how.

'Sherman, cover this end,' Angel said, ignoring the marshal's reaction to his wound. It wasn't as bad as it looked, although he could feel the first faint, flickering flutters of warning weakness inside his head. There was a point when your body could no longer be pushed by adrenalin: the shock came up like a tide rising on the Continental Shelf, irresistible, consuming, total — and then you went down. He knew that would come, but he wanted the man who had tried to kill him before it did.

'I'll take the far end,' Hogben said.

'You all right, Angel?'

Angel nodded. With fingers which fumbled very slightly, a fumbling he did not allow them to see, he reloaded his six-gun.

'All right,' he said. 'I'm all right.'

'Let me go, man,' Sherman said. 'Or Mike.'

'No,' Angel said, flatly. 'I want this one alive.'

'For God's sake wait, then,' Sherman snapped. 'I can get a dozen men down here to flush him out!'

'I don't have the time,' Angel told him. Sherman nodded, thinking he meant the waiting train, the long haul to Trinidad still to be made. Angel let him think it.

Without another word he slid around the edge of the carriage shed and into its gloomy interior. It was simply a pair of walls with a timber roof, open at both ends, with three sets of buffers up against the brush-choked bank of the western end of the yard. Hogben would be down at that end; if the killer tried to bolt that way, he wouldn't get far.

There were three lines of track inside the shed. On the pair nearest Angel was a row of four coal trucks. The center line was empty. On the far side of the shed were two passenger coaches. He flattened himself on the ground, his eyes already accustomed to the gloom, scouring the spaces between the bogies for a pair of boots or legs. Nothing. The man wasn't that much of a fool.

And he still had a carbine.

He eased his way along the line of coal trucks to the far end of the shed. The light was better now, and halfway down he found a big old packing case, nearly three feet high, that had obviously brought in some mining machinery or maybe a lathe for one of the sawmills up in the Rio Chama country. He eased himself behind it, and using the wall as a brace, slid up onto the top of the case. He put his six-gun beneath his armpit under the coat and cocked it, the triple click deadened, almost inaudible. Then he quickly stood, his gaze sweeping the length of the high-sided coal trucks. The truck at the end had a tarpaulin loosely spread inside it, and he swept the gun up and fired three shots into it. He dropped quickly and waited.

The thunder of the shots magnified by the closed space sounded like the crack of doom. The gun-smoke swirled and drifted in the uncertain breeze. Angel shook his head. He eased himself back, getting into a position where he could slide down to the ground. The whiplashing crack of the Winchester blended with the smashing impact of the bullets hitting the crate inches from his face, whacking huge splinters out of the wood. One of them flickered across his face like a razor, drawing a fine-etched line that oozed blood into the corner of his mouth. He found himself on the ground, having rolled off the top of the crate without even knowing it. There was a deep, solid throbbing in his head now, and for a moment he had trouble focusing his eyes. He didn't even know where the shots had come from. But there was only one place left.

He laughed like a hunting wolf and rolled onto his haunches, the six-gun still ready in his hand. Then he ran fast for the end of the carriage shed, coming around the coal wagons in a diving forward somersault. Like a rolling ball, he barreled across the graveled space between the rails as the man in the far passenger coach, his carbine leveled out of the window, poured five simultaneous shots at the fleeting target. Then Angel was sheltered by the end of the coach, and he swung aboard. The door into the carriage was open, the interior dark but visible.

What would the killer expect — roof or interior?

Roof.

He nodded and slid into the doorway, moving on silent feet the length of the carriage. When he came to the vestibule, which led into the platform outside, he stopped and slid between two seats on the right-hand side, gently lowering the window. It slid down silently and he leaned out, his hand arching up and over, tossing his six-gun up high onto the roof of the next carriage.

Vargas heard the sound on the roof that he had been expecting. He was poised by the platform between the two carriages, and he went through the door like a snake, eeling down onto the gravel with the cocked carbine up and leveled for the killing shot at the exposed figure he expected to see on the roof of the carriage.

His jaw was just dropping with the realization that there was no one there when Angel landed lightly behind him. He was nicely set as Vargas whirled around, his hand already clenched in the way that Kee Lai had taught him during those endless, punishing sessions they had shared in the gloomy gymnasium the Justice Department shared with the army. The Korean had taught him that there is an inner strength upon which a man can call, summoning all of himself at one moment, directing all that is him into the effort he needs to make. The Korean had called it *ch'i* and said there was no word for it in the English language. But Angel knew that it was a total belief in yourself — if all of you was at its fullest potential, what you were and what you could do were insuperable, unstoppable. Thus he knew that when he hit Vargas with the inward, downward chopping, clenched hand, it would break the man. And it did.

The Mexican was driven to his knees as if a pile driver had hit him, a thin scream of agony wrenched from his twisted mouth. The carbine clattered to the gravel from his nerveless hands, and he pitched forward, writhing in agony on the ground while Angel looked dispassionately down as if the man were some form of lizard he had trodden upon. He felt no pity for the man, nothing. Academically there was a corner of his mind which knew, as if turning the pages of some bizarre medical catalog, that he had probably broken Vargas's collarbone and shoulder blade, dislocated or snapped the humerus, crushed or punctured the upper lung, cracked or broken two or more ribs, and possibly punctured the pleura. Medically Vargas was in desperate need of a doctor, not because he would die, but because without the proper attention, his injuries could cause him great pain and suffering, possible hemorrhage and pleurisy or pneumonia aggravated by massive shock. He shouted two names and slowly looked up as Sherman and Hogben came running into the shed, guns drawn. They saw the twisting, writhing thing on the floor, and both men looked at Angel's empty holster and unarmed hands.

'This man will need a doctor,' Angel said.

'So will you,' Hogben told him grimly.

'I don't have time,' Angel said.

Then he went down.

14

'You're out of your head,' the doctor said.

'Uh-huh,' Angel replied, struggling a little with the buttons on his shirt.

His right hand was a little stiff, and his entire right side was a huge purpled mass of bruised, iodine-painted, tightly bandaged tissue. He felt a little uncomfortable, but all right. Not first class. All right. He buttoned his shirt and reached for his pants.

'You ought to stay in bed for a week,' the doctor persisted. 'If those stitches burst . . . ' He shuddered theatrically at the thought.

'I seem to be saying this a lot,' Angel told him. 'But I don't have the time.'

'All right, Mister Angel,' the doctor said, throwing up his hands. 'You've convinced me. You're made of whale-bone and rawhide, spring steel and hickory. Bullets bounce off you, and strong men break their hands trying to hurt you. Knock you down and up you get, good as new. Like hell! You put any real strain on those stitches, and they'll pop open like a clam in a kettle.'

'I'll be sure to come back for you to do it over personally and tell me you told me so,' grinned Angel. 'How's Vargas, by the way?'

'He'll live,' the gray-haired man told him. 'He's probably in better shape than you. They tell me you did all that with your hands. Is that right?' When Angel didn't reply, he shook his head. 'He'll be lucky if he ever uses that left hand properly again.'

'He won't need to where he's going,' Angel said, coldly. 'Thanks for everything, Doc.'

The doctor shook his head.

'They tell me you work for the Department of Justice,' he said. 'They must be quite an organization.'

'I guess you could say they are,' Angel grinned.

'Take care, Angel,' the older man said, resting a gentle hand on his arm. 'Try not to put too much strain on your right side. You'll probably forget what I've told you as soon as you walk out of here, but try not to. You might keel over at the worst possible moment — for you.'

Angel nodded and went out. The doctor's warmly furnished adobe was on Palace Avenue, right across the street from the Federal Building, where Sherman's office was situated. Sheriff Hogben was waiting outside for him, a buckboard standing ready to take him back down to the depot.

'If at first you don't succeed,' Hogben said, smiling.

'Don't be dumb, give up,' Angel said wryly. 'I've lost a lot of time, Mike.'

'Not too much,' Hogben said, pulling his fat watch from its nest in his waistcoat pocket 'I make it just after one.'

'Five hours,' Angel said. 'We could've been up around Springer by now.'

'You should have heard old Bob Gray complainin',' Hogben chuckled. 'After he done all that work, billy-be-damned if he didn't have to do her all over. He like to bust a gut!'

Despite himself, Angel grinned at the image. He climbed into the buckboard, and Hogben gigged the horses into a trot around the plaza. It was a bright autumn day, and the round adobes surrounding the square looked golden and brown, as if they were sugarcoated, their windows fat currants in the dumpy cakes of the houses. They passed the sprawling La Fonda and clopped across Water Street.

'Y'ever see the Miraculous Staircase, Frank?' Hogben asked.

'The what?'

'The Miraculous Staircase,' Hogben explained. 'It's in a chapel down on the left there, along Water Street.'

'Why miraculous?'

'Aw, some old legend. They was buildin' a chapel down there, see, an' for some reason the workmen gave up

191

on tryin' to build a staircase from the ground up to the choir loft. Too difficult, they said, or some such thing. Stood for a long while, sort of half-done, then one day a feller comes along, says he's a carpenter an' he'll finish the job. Built this beautiful circular staircase.'

'And?'

'Well, that's the thing. I've seen it, Frank. Fitted together like *that*, you never saw work like it. And not a nail in the whole damn thing. It hangs together with nothin' holdin' it up as far as anyone can see. Mexicans reckon it was Saint Joseph built it.'

'Saint Joseph?'

'Yeah, the Good Lord's old man. Whoever he was, the man who built it disappeared without a trace. Never asked for payment. Never seen again.'

'It's a good story,' Angel said.

'Yeah,' Hogben agreed, and he swung the team around in front of the railroad depot. John Sherman came forward, smiling.

'I've telegraphed Washington on your behalf,' he said. 'And Cecil Smith up in Trinidad. They know you've been delayed a little, but not why.'

'Good,' Angel nodded. 'I'm thanking you.'

'*De nada*,' Sherman said, as they shook hands. 'Although,' he added with a grin, 'you might at least acknowledge the good work I did in keeping Bob Gray away from the depot. He was just bustin' to tell you how much trouble you'd caused him.'

'I bet,' Angel grinned. 'Take good care of Vargas.'

'No sweat,' the marshal said.

Angel shook hands with Hogben, swung around, and moved quickly through the shaded depot building and out into the passenger bay. The engine which had been ready earlier in the day was at the platform now, hissing slightly as if impatient. The same engineer was leaning out of the same window with the same resigned expression on his face. It didn't change as Angel stopped below him and told him his name.

'Howdy,' the engineer said. 'Get yourself aboard.'

Angel swung up onto the footplate, and the engineer took hold of the brake handle. It looked like the handle on some gigantic coffee grinder. The heat from the roaring furnace was like a physical blow as the stoker knocked it open with his shovel and slid another shovelful of coal on top of the glowing fires inside.

'How long you figure it will take us to get to Trinidad?' Angel shouted, as the engineer released the brake and the locomotive made a thundering metallic noise, shuddering like some huge animal and then easing gently and easily backward out of the depot.

'Something over two hundred miles,' the engineer said, giving a tug on a dangling cord that released a mighty whoosing whistle. He did it again, scratching his chin and watching the startled doves wheeling in a panicked half-circle above the roof of the depot.

'With nothing to pull? That's an interestin' question, lad.'

He scratched his chin and watched the stoker check the boiler.

'Not too much now, Paddy,' he warned. 'You don't want to blow us up.'

The stoker grinned, showing gaping holes where most of his teeth should have been. The engineer shook his head.

'It's all them potatoes, you know,' he whispered loudly. Paddy grinned again.

'Now as to your question. If we can somehow coax this old cow,' he patted the side of the engine fondly, 'to run that long, we might do it in six hours. Of course, we might coax her to do it faster, in which case, I might say less. But then of course — '

'It might take longer,' Angel guessed.

'Now that's true,' the engineer said. He rubbed his chin ruefully. 'The thing is, ye see. The thing is, it's never been done, this. So there's no way of knowing. The ordinary train now, that would take nine, ten hours or more, depending on conditions. But like this. Just an engine, a tender. A clear line with nothing in the way. Nobody knows, ye see.'

The depot was falling away behind them. Angel thought he could see Sherman and Hogben standing on the platform, but he couldn't be sure.

'I'll bet you fifty dollars you can't do it in six hours,' Angel said to the engineer.

'Now that's interestin', that is,' the engineer said. 'Wouldn't ye say, Paddy?'

Paddy gave his gap-toothed grin and swung another shovelful of coal into the furnace.

'Aye,' the engineer said, with a thoughtful look on his face as he opened up the throttle and headed the engine downhill toward Lamy.

★ ★ ★

Angel lost his bet. They got into Trinidad just eighteen minutes after eight o'clock in the evening after the

196

most astonishing journey Angel had ever experienced. He had watched with awe as the engineer, Tim Wilton, and his Irish stoker had spelled each other, working in smooth unison that only comes from mutual respect, nursing every ounce of power from the thundering engine. They took her slowly up the grades into the Glorieta and then down out of the seven thousand-foot pass toward the long northern curve at Bernal at giddying, rocking, reckless speeds that threatened to hurl them from the tracks. Angel watched the landmarks fly past, astonished at how quickly they loomed on the horizon, drew level, and then after what seemed like nothing more than minutes, fell astern of the thundering machine. The incessant hammering rhythm and *clickatter-clickatter* of the wheels bore in upon the brain until the brain became unconscious of them. Their eyes grew red-rimmed and sore from flying cinders and rushing wind, their faces lightly coated with grime from the boiler and soot from the streaming banner of smoke which marked their hurtling passage. They roared over the Gallinas and through Las Vegas, startling horses hitched near the depot buildings. Across the Mora, the Turkey Mountains looming on their left — he was reminded of the scattered sprawl of Fort Union and the men he knew there — then into the beginning of the gradient that would lead them up and up and up again to the almost eight thousand foot height of the Raton Pass. Wilton eased the throttle back a little now, causing the pistons to slow just enough so that someone who had been listening to them for several hours could tell the difference. Springer sprawled like scattered boxes on the rolling brown plain off to the right as they rocked across the wooden trestle bridges spanning the Cimarron. Way off to the northwest Angel could see the towering peaks of the Sangre de Cristos, the pink snow mantling the jagged horns of the range that had given them their name — the mountains of the blood of Christ. Thirty miles to the east he could see Laughlin Peak, Tinaja lying lower and to the north. Behind those tumbling heights lay Kiowa and the Palo Blanco, where the ruined fortress of an insane man lay forgotten in the wilderness.

The darkness was coming down now, and the long searching beam of the locomotive's single eye cut a long tunnel of light up and along the right-of-way ahead. The thickening pines cast ghostly shades as the train thundered by, and above the glowing funnel a cloud of sparks flickered and swirled, dying in the night like falling fireflies. The sound of their passage was a dull, throbbing, ceaseless thunder in their ears as they rushed through deeply scoured cuttings in solid rock, hurtling between stands of indifferent mountain aspen and larch.

Raton lay ahead, and in a moment they passed its gleaming lights in the depot and the men on the platform watching their passage, their faces outlined strangely by the lights. Then they were in darkness again and moving faster.

'Twenty miles,' Tim Wilton said, wiping his face with a rag that left a two-inch wide smear of oil across it. 'An' all of it downhill!'

He smiled triumphantly at Angel and produced a turnip watch the size of a child's hand. 'Seven-farty-five,' Wilton said, grinning. 'What d'ye make of that, Paddy?'

Paddy looked up with his broken grin, and he was still grinning when they pulled into Trinidad thirty-three minutes later.

★ ★ ★

He was on the depot platform when the train came in. She rolled downhill into the station, her brightly-lit cars rolling slowly past, the engine wheezing and clanking to a stop. The big man watched each window, checking each face from the shadowed recess where he stood with his left hand lightly touching the concealed butt of the short-barreled Colt's pocket pistol. He had checked methodically but quietly; the clerk at the depot ticket window had assured him no 'specials' had come in from Sante Fe that day, nor right up to this moment. So if Angel was not on this train, then Angel was dead.

There were swirls of movement as people called to each other. Women ran with arms outspread toward husbands or lovers. Men clapped other men on the shoulder, their voices loudly cheerful and self-conscious.

The big man held himself carefully in check, not moving; watching, watching.

In fifteen minutes the train would pull out, but this time in two halves. The forward three carriages, linked to a new engine, would climb north through Pueblo and Colorado Springs to Denver and then on to Cheyenne. The rear ones would turn eastward, running all the way downhill to La Junta and across the endless drab flatness of the Kansas plains through Dodge and Wichita and onward to journey's end in Kansas City. Still he did not move. The people who had gotten off the train were dispersing now, the porters either following them laden with luggage or stacking trunks on iron-wheeled trolleys. There were a few new faces standing around — men saying good-bye to business acquaintances and a woman with two children being helped up the steps by a drummer carrying a sample case.

No Angel.

The train jerked as the couplings were parted, and he could hear the second engine chuntering across from the siding farther down the track.

Five minutes to go, perhaps. Not much more.

And no Angel.

Then Angel was dead. There was no question about it. If Angel had been alive, he would have been here by now.

If he had baited any trap, he would have sprung it. He felt some regret. It was hard to think of Angel dead. He emerged from his shadowed corner and went into the depot, walking confidently to the baggage counter. The man behind the counter was young and fresh, and he looked at the big man incuriously.

'It's a leather suitcase,' he was told, as the big man pushed a yellow ticket across the counter toward him. The ticket had been torn, and was patched with adhesive tape. 'Hurry, please, I have to catch that train.'

'Yessir,' the clerk said.

He went back among the shelves and came out carrying a fat suitcase with a worn leather handle.

'This the one, sir?' he asked.

'Let me see,' the big man said. He checked the ticket pasted on the side of the bag: the number matched the one he had memorized through hours of staring waiting. 'Yes, this is it.'

'Two dollars to pay, sir,' the clerk

said. Everything was normal. The air held no threat.

The big man took a wallet from the breast pocket of his black Prince Albert frock coat and paid over the two dollars. He picked up the bag and hurried out of the baggage room. He was still cautious, checking left and right along the platform as he came out of the doorway. No one even looked at him. Most of the passengers were already aboard, and one or two people were hanging out of windows, waiting for the train to pull out. He hurried along the platform to the front carriage, swinging up onto the train and entering the warm, brightly lit compartment. The engine in front gave a shuddering snort as he settled into a vacant seat by the left-hand window. He took out his watch. They were late leaving.

And then a familiar voice shattered his composure.

'Hello, Angus,' Angel said.

15

Angus Wells smiled. 'I should have known,' he said softly. There was no defeat in his voice, just a faint hint at amusement with himself, of self-chastisement, the voice of a man mildly annoyed with himself for a repeated folly.

'What made you think you could get away with it, Angus?' Angel asked.

'What makes you think I haven't?'

'Look in the suitcase,' Angel suggested. He saw the effect of his words, the brief flaring in Wells's confident eyes quickly masked. Wells sat there and shook his head, concentrating on keeping the sour taste of failure from turning into vomit.

'You're bluffing,' he whispered.

'That's right,' Angel said. 'Open the suitcase and see.'

'No,' Wells said. He put the suitcase

down on the seat beside him, looking at the man opposite him. He remembered the kid in the hospital at Fort Bowie shouting '*You can, Angus!*' Just yesterday? He listened to the sound of his blood surging in his veins, a rising, throbbing pulse of growing anger which increased steadily, rapidly, constantly, measuredly, and ever more tangibly inside his head until he could feel the big vein on the side of his throat swelling, feel his brain flood with the rage at his own failure, the failure of it all.

'Well,' he said, levelly, controlling himself. 'Have you got me — or have I got you?'

'I'll have to take you back, Angus,' Angel said, as though the question was simple. It's serious, Frank, Wells thought.

'I could have killed you half a dozen times,' he said. 'Half a dozen times.'

'You should have,' Angel told him.

'The Mexicans?'

'Two dead, one alive. He'll talk.'

'Ah,' Wells said. 'That, too.' He did

not want to kill Frank Angel. Maybe he wouldn't have to. But he would. One part of him wanted to kill him right now. Not because of the money: that part of it was over, done. But because it was him. Because it was Angel.

'You'll want my gun,' he said. Frank Angel nodded, his eyes wary.

'Easy,' he said.

'Yes,' Wells replied. He touched the butt of the gun in his special holster and it sprung into his hand. For a millisecond he was tempted by the reassuring feeling in his palm, but when he looked at Angel's hand, he saw a gun in it. He hadn't seen Frank Angel move; but there was the six-gun, solid and deadly, leveled at his belly. He shrugged and tried to manage a smile, which slid off one side of his face as he handed over the pocket pistol.

'Frank,' he said. 'I'm going to stand up.'

'Do it slowly,' Angel advised. A woman in the opposite seat had seen the gun and was staring at it.

'Listen to me,' Wells said. 'I'm going to stand up and walk off this train.'

'No,' Angel said. 'No you're not.'

'You've got my gun, Frank,' Wells said. His smile was tentative, but it stayed on this time, grew bolder.

'Don't,' Angel pleaded with him. 'Please, Angus.'

'It'll have to be in the back, Frank,' Wells said. He got up very, very slowly, and Frank Angel watched him. 'If you can do it.'

'Don't make me,' the younger man said. His voice was urgent now.

'If you do it, do it right,' Wells said. He turned around quickly and for a long, long moment he waited for the sound of the hammer of the six-gun. Then he stepped forward and walked, without haste, down the length of the carriage.

'Wells!' Angel shouted.

Without turning, Angus Wells stepped off the train and onto the platform. As he did so, a man with a star gleaming on his coat came out of the doorway of the baggage room. His gun was in his holster, but his hand was on it. There was puzzlement on his face. He looked inside the carriage and saw Angel standing alone in the middle of the aisle with the six-gun in his hand, and then he turned toward Wells, pulling the gun, but he was much, much too late.

The little derringer that Wells had shaken from his sleeve holster boomed, a bright yellow flower of flame blossoming from the stubby barrel. The sheriff was slammed back into the doors of the baggage room, smashing them open, the glass on one side shivering into fragments that clamored on the stone platform as they fell. A woman was screaming, and the young man who had been behind the counter came out through the doors with a cocked gun in his hand, staring wildly left and right. He saw Wells running at the far end of the platform and threw a shot without aiming that fragmented one of the glass globes on the oil lamps lighting the platform.

The young man was the son and deputy of the Trinidad sheriff, who lay dying in a spreading pool of black blood on the floor of the baggage room. He ran fast toward the end of the platform from which Wells had jumped as Angel swung down from the train. There was a commotion inside the carriage, and people were pulling down windows to try and see what was happening.

'Get back inside!' Angel yelled, running along the platform after the shirt-sleeved deputy. He heard the six-gun boom as the young man jumped from the end of the platform, and then he was behind the deputy, who whirled with the six-gun. He was panting as if he had run several hundred yards uphill, his breath wheezing in his throat. The hand holding the six-gun was trembling, and Angel gently pushed it aside.

'He . . . ' the young man sobbed. 'He . . . '

'I know,' Angel said. 'I saw it.'

'You . . . ' The deputy looked at him with eyes full of disgust. 'You . . . saw it! You . . . you let him walk off that train and . . . and kill my . . . father!'

'No,' Angel said, meaning, no it wasn't like that at all. He wanted the young man to know why he hadn't been able to shoot Angus Wells in the back, but he said no more because there was no way he could tell the boy.

He didn't even know himself.

He touched the deputy's arm.

'Tell them to hold the train,' he said. 'I'm going to look for him.'

The deputy looked at him with lacklustre eyes. The reaction was hitting him now. Later, he would be brave again and tell them how he'd chased the killer. 'Tell them,' Angel said. 'And get that suitcase off the train. It's got a quarter of a million dollars in it.'

The youngster nodded. He looked at the six-gun in his hand as if he had never seen it before and then jammed it into the waistband of his pants. He climbed back up onto the rough stone platform, and Angel watched him walk back toward the pools of light in the center of the depot where the train stood.

Now, he thought. Where? Where would he go? Where would I go if I were him? He stood there and thought the way he had been taught to think, the way he knew that Wells had been taught to think, because Wells had taught him.

When you want to hide something, hide it openly. Someone searching for what you have hidden, someone at least as intelligent as you, will look in all the places you can invent and others you have not thought of. So hide whatever you must hide as if it were useless, valueless, worthless. And the seeker will often overlook it. Not always. But often. If you are pursued, your pursuer expects one thing — that you will run. The pursuer will be looking for you ahead of him, for that is where he expects you to be. If he is an intelligent hunter, he will anticipate your doubling and bisect the circle you are trying to make, thus ending the hunt. So you must play not fox, but human fox. The one place the hunter knows the fox will not go while he is being hunted is his lair, the place he most wants to protect. If you will outwit the hunter, go where he is sure you will not be and where he will not think to seek you.

Of course.

He got back on the platform and went toward the knot of men standing beneath the lamps in the center and outside the shattered doors of the baggage room. They had carried the sheriff's body away. There was a dusty black smear on the stone.

'Lost him,' Angel told them, his voice emotionless. 'Can't see a damned thing out there.'

The men on the platform just looked at him and said nothing. One of them had the leather suitcase in his hand.

'Better let the train go,' Angel told

the stationmaster. 'No point in holdin' these folks up any longer.' He pointed to the valise. 'Put that somewhere safe.'

'Uh-huh,' the man said. The stationmaster slipped a watch out of his waistcoat pocket and looked at it and then at Angel, as though saying he hoped Angel realized that he was responsible for how late the train was. Then he went over to the trolley standing by the wall and picked up the flickering bulls-eye lantern.

'Board!' he shouted. His voice sounded strange, thin, and ghostly. There was a faint hint of mist from the hidden mountains off to the west, and the stationmaster's breath billowed like smoke as he shouted. 'Denver train, stoppin' at Pueblo and Colorado Springs.'

The conductor stepped down from the caboose and swung his lantern in reply to the stationmaster's. They waved at each other, and then the conductor turned his lamp around so that the green light flared in the darkness. The engineer pulled his whistle cord and the big engine *shun-shun-shun-shunned*, trembling perceptibly as the huge drive wheels bit against the steel rails.

The train was moving gently, easily, and quickly forward now, and Angel placed his bet, swinging up onto the rear observation platform as the caboose swung by, the conductor watching his lithe maneuver with startled eyes.

'Uh — what the hell?' he began, his chin coming up.

'You a betting man?' Angel asked, his grin mirthless and taut. He was taking a damned long chance, and he knew it.

'Uh, what?' the conductor asked. 'Uh, nope, cain't say as I am.'

'Pity,' Angel said. 'Or I'd have bet you I wasn't the last one who was going to swing onto here tonight.'

'Uh?' the conductor said.

'Forget it,' Angel told him. 'It wasn't much of a joke, anyway.'

'Sure,' the conductor said, humoring

him. He opened the door leading into the caboose and went inside. The train moved across the rails toward the main line spur at the northern edge of town.

Angel waited.

16

'Well, well,' Frank Angel said to no one in particular.

They had only come perhaps four or five hundred yards when the train started to slow down noticeably. Angel tried to recall the layout of Trinidad in the filing index of his memory, the long S of the street with the opera house at its center, the looping curve in the road at the southern edge of town which seemed to have been put there as an introduction to the snaking twists of the Raton Pass that lay ahead. The northern edge, the northern edge! Was there a bridge over the tracks? There was. He remembered it. The trail rose from the valley of the Picketwire, as local people called the Purgatoire River, and turned right over a solid, rumbling wooden bridge. Off to the right the Y-shaped switch with its centrally located box turned the oncoming trains left for Denver or right for La junta.

The train was almost at walking pace now as they came up the deep cutting that lay to the west of the town. Leaning carefully out, he saw the looming bulk of the big bridge above the train, its blackness more solid, more real than the blackness of the night. The engineer applied his brakes, and the train came to a slowing halt. The engineer waited until his wheels picked up the switch before he opened his throttle again. *Calicka-calack* went the wheels. *Calicka-calack.*

Then he saw the running figure, and Angel knew he had been right.

Wells came away from the deeper shadows of the cutting wall, quartering across the tracks toward the center of the train. His limp was very pronounced, and for a brief second, Angel felt a touch of sorrow, of pity for the running man. Then he called his name.

Angus Wells came to a startled stop in the middle of the open space on the far side of the switch box, exposed by the light of the lamps burning above him. He saw Angel as Angel swung down to the ground and moved toward him, and he gave a roar of anger. Angel kept coming with his six-gun up and let Wells have a chance to run. But Wells wasn't running. All of his frustrated rage swelled into one pulsating roar of killing lust, blanking out his animal cunning, his instinct to survive, leaving nothing but the need to kill the man in front of him. He came at Angel hard, low, and fast, his head down. Angel waited, with the gun ready, poised on the balls of his feet, unable to believe Wells was this stupid. Still the big man came on at him, and Angel eared back the hammer of the six-gun. Then Wells was level with a high pile of block gravel left for grading work by the gandy dancers, and he threw himself behind it in a veering, arching leap, the derringer in his hand spurting flame as he went over the shoulder of the gravel pile and rolled out of sight behind it. It was a brilliant maneuver, and if he had been using a six-gun instead of the tiny pocket pistol, whose effective range was no more than a few yards, he would have probably killed Frank Angel there and then. But the unrifled ball whistled a good two feet away from its target. Angel was already moving forward now in a running crouch, the gun deadly and level, with no thought of hesitation. If he saw Wells now, he would kill him. Wells knew it now too, and when Angel came skittering around the gravel pile with the six-gun ready, Wells had a two-handed grip on the shovel that had been lying on the pile. Wells swung it in a whistling, biting arch into Angels right side, and Angel yelled a shout of agony as the heavy metal blade glanced off his tensed right arm and smashed into his wounded side. The blow took Angel off his feet as if he had been roped from a running horse, whacking him sideways, his six-gun flipping out of his hand and landing with a soft thud somewhere in the darkness. He cried out as he hit the ground, feeling the soft tearing pain as the stitches in his side burst apart. Warm wetness spread along his side, and for a moment he was a child again in a warm bed, his senses dislocated. Wells came at him again now with the shovel upraised and the edge turned this time to cut, smashing it down at Angel, who desperately arched his body away. The shovel clanged on the railway line, and the force of the impact twisted the shovel out of Wells's grasp. Angel was on his feet now, and he struck at Wells with his right hand. He might as well have tried to knock the man down with a wet rag — his arm would not respond to his brain's commands, and he saw Well's left hand move up and across from the right shoulder. He turned himself desperately to parry the blow that would kill him if it landed. The edge of Wells's hand, hardened to the toughness of a brick, glanced off Angel's shoulder and against his forehead, jarring his head back. Angel reeled away, almost falling again, his right hand banging almost useless at his side.

'Come on!' Wells said. 'Come on, Angel!' Come and be killed, he meant.

Angel shook his head to clear it. His side was slippery with fresh blood, and he could feel the swaying dizziness which precedes a blackout. *You might keel over at the worst possible moment — for you*, he could hear the doctor in Sante Fe say.

Wells came at him again, hard this time, and Angel had no time to do more than parry. He stopped the chopping blow and skipped back. Wells hissed with frustration.

Survive! The first rule they taught you. It doesn't matter how. There are no rules other than the first rule: survive! He slid his left hand down to the secret scabbard in his boots between the outer leather and the inner lining. Inside it, concealed from casual search by the mule-ear straps, nestled a flat-bladed Solingen steel throwing knife, mate to the one on the right-hand side. They had been specially made for him, as had the boots which concealed them, by the armorer at the Justice Department. And they were his last chance. Wells saw his movement, and came in again, grinning like a wolf pulling down a baby calf. His right leg lashed out, and the knife flickered away into the darkness.

'What now, Angel?' he jeered. 'The belt buckle?'

Then he reached up behind his neck, and from a scabbard which hung on a loop around his throat, he slid a knife, long and two-edged, its needle point a wicked diamond glinting in the thin light of the switch box lamps. Wells palmed the knife like an expert — flat on his hand, the blade lying between forefinger and thumb — lightly holding it like a sword. Angel watched him weave and sway, his eyes always on the hand with the knife in it, never leaving it, forcing himself to concentrate on it.

Suddenly, Wells slashed at him, the

knife whipping audibly through the air, inches from Angel's belly as he sprang back. Again Wells slashed and then suddenly back again. Angel felt the beaded sweat on his forehead cold in the night air and knew he was afraid. If he tried to get the other knife from his boot on the right, Wells would kill him while he was trying for it. If he did not, Wells would kill him anyway.

There wasn't much of anything left. In a few more moments Angel knew his eyesight would start to blur, and he would see Wells move too late, and he would be dead on the dirty sand. *If you are pursued, your pursuer expects one thing: that you will run.*

He stopped and forced his breathing inward, directing all of himself to this place, at this moment, perhaps for this last time. In his mind's eye he saw the slanting eyes of Kee Lai. He summoned that inner power the Korean had called *ch'i* until he felt the strength come into him, flow through him, warm his genitals.

'All right,' he said brokenly. 'All right. Finish it.'

Wells's head came up, and he peered at Angel. Angel let his head hang, and he saw the flickering feint with the knife, waiting, watching Wells from beneath his eyebrows. Another flickering feint. This time the blade drew blood from his unprotected arm. Wells giggled, sure now.

'Angel?' he said.

Wells came closer to get a better look, and Angel put all of himself into the terrible movement of his foot. The kick came up off the ground with every ounce of strength he had left in him and buried itself in Wells's groin with a cracking thud. Wells screamed like a pig in a slaughterhouse, a mangled, banshee shriek that bounced off the stone walls of the railway cutting and echoed back as he went over on his face, his hands buried in his mangled crotch, back arching against the agony of what was broken inside him. Everything seemed to be moving in slow motion now, and Angel watched Wells go down as if he was underwater, legs flailing, mouth distended in one long continuous scream that went on and on and on until Angel slid the second knife out of his boot with blood-slippery fingers and stopped it.

17

'I still can't believe it,' the attorney general said.

'No, sir,' Frank Angel replied dutifully.

He was fit again now. Tomorrow he would be going to the hospital to have the second lot of stitches taken out of his side, which had healed well — no damned thanks to him, the surgeon had said, tutting and fussing over the ragged wound.

'What made him think he could get away with it?' the man behind the desk asked of nobody in particular. His voice was full of grief.

'I asked him that,' Angel said. 'He never did say.'

'But why?' the older man persisted. 'Why, in God's name, why?'

'I think I can answer that, sir,' Angel said. 'A man like Angus Wells, he'd bitterly resent being put out to pasture. He knew he was as good a man with one arm and one leg as most other men are with two. As I damned well found out.'

'But the medical report . . . '

'Medical reports don't stretch to cover a man's pride,' Angel said quietly. 'It was Wells's pride that was hurt, and when he realized he had a way to steal a quarter of a million dollars of the government's money, it must have seemed like a delightful irony. Irresistible. Especially when he could cover himself so well. Who would suspect the Justice Department's chief investigator if he asked for details about the shipment? Who would question his appearing anywhere, asking whatever he wanted to know, doing whatever he wanted to do?'

'Like intercepting your telegraph messages, you mean?'

'For one thing,' Angel agreed. 'By the way, I've attended to that clerk in Las Vegas. He'll have plenty of time to think over what he did while he's in prison.'

'As long as we didn't know where you were, then we wouldn't try to contact you.'

'And by definition, I wouldn't know that Wells was not in Washington. I thought I saw him when we made the break out of the penitentiary, but I wasn't sure, even when I was nicked by a bullet. I'd asked them to make it look good. I reckon Wells was trying to make it look even better.'

'But it was a clumsy job, Angel,' the attorney general said. 'Badly planned, clumsily executed. He hadn't a chance of getting away with it from the moment you reached Santa Fe. Once we knew your suspicions, it would only have been a matter of time before we took him.'

'It was always only a matter of time,' Angel said. 'It didn't matter to Wells if we knew — in fact, I think he almost wanted us to know — as long as he got to Trinidad before me and picked up the suitcase. He was very cool, you know. He anticipated everything I'd do right up to the end. Knew I'd telegraph through and put a watch on the suitcase: left it sitting there for two clear days until he thought I was dead. If I had been dead, there wouldn't have been a damned thing they could have done to stop him picking it up. He'd have shown them department identification and overruled any local law. Picked up the money and run.'

'We would still have caught him — eventually,' the attorney general maintained stoutly.

'I wonder,' Angel said. 'I'm not so sure.'

'Well,' the attorney general said, his voice tired. 'I've got more work to do. Reports to write. We don't often have someone in this department go bad.'

Angel said nothing. There wasn't anything to say. He knew the old man and Wells had been friends. He had thought of Angus as a friend himself. He thought of that insane fight in the shadowed railway cutting. Friend?

The attorney general pressed the bell on his desk that summoned his personal private secretary, Amabel Rowe. Angel got up from his chair, nodding hello. She smiled back, and he thought he saw something secret behind the smile.

'Well, off you go, my boy,' the attorney general said. 'When do they take out the stitches?'

'Tomorrow, sir,' Angel replied.

'Good. You'll be taking a short rest, a day or two, before you report back?'

'If that's in order, sir.'

'Certainly, certainly. Got anything in mind?'

Frank Angel made absolutely certain he couldn't see Amabel Rowe's face, nor she his, as he replied.

'Yes, sir, I have. Aim to take a beautiful woman to dinner, buy her champagne, take her for a carriage ride in the moonlight.'

'Capital, capital,' chortled the attorney general. 'Enjoy yourself, my boy. You've earned it.'

Amabel Rowe opened the door, and Frank Angel went out into the anteroom.

'Real champagne?' she whispered.

'Is there any other kind?' he replied.

She closed the door, smiling.

THE END